SUGARHOUSE
TRIALS

LENORE SYLVAIN DEXTER

Copyright © 2021 Immerser

All rights reserved.

This book or any portion thereof may not be reproduced or used in any manner whatsoever without the express written permission of the author except for the use of brief quotations in a book review.

Although this book is largely fictional, it is based on some true events. Where facts and evidence were not obtainable, the author has used imagination to bridge the gaps. Some names have been changed to protect individual identities.

Printed in the United States of America.

ISBN: 978-1-7354660-2-6

First Edition, 2021

I dedicate this book to my husband, Joe. Without his input, I would never have been able to write this story.

TABLE OF CONTENTS

Prologue 1

PART ONE

Chapter One 9
Chapter Two 17
Chapter Three 25
Chapter Four 31
Chapter Five 37
Chapter Six 39
Chapter Seven 47
Chapter Eight 51
Chapter Nine 53
Chapter Ten 55
Chapter Eleven 61
Chapter Twelve 65
Chapter Thirteen 71
Chapter Fourteen 79
Chapter Fifteen 83
Chapter Sixteen 87
Chapter Seventeen 93
Chapter Eighteen 97

PART TWO

Chapter Nineteen 107
Chapter Twenty 111
Chapter Twenty-One 127

PART THREE

Chapter Twenty-Two 133
Chapter Twenty-Three 141
Chapter Twenty-Four 145
Chapter Twenty-Five 149
Chapter Twenty-Six 153
Chapter Twenty-Seven 159
Chapter Twenty-Eight 163
Chapter Twenty-Nine 169
Chapter Thirty 175
Chapter Thirty-One 179
Chapter Thirty-Two 185
Chapter Thirty-Three 189

PART FOUR

Chapter Thirty-Four 195
Chapter Thirty-Five 197
Chapter Thirty-Six 201
Chapter Thirty-Seven 205
Chapter Thirty-Eight 207
Chapter Thirty-Nine 211
Chapter Forty 213
Chapter Forty-One 217
Chapter Forty-Two 219
Chapter Forty-Three 223
Chapter Forty-Four 225
Chapter Forty-Five 227

Chapter Forty-Six 231
Chapter Forty-Seven 235
Chapter Forty-Eight...237
Chapter Forty-Nine..241
Chapter Fifty..249

PART FIVE

Chapter Fifty-One 255
Chapter Fifty-Two..259
Chapter Fifty-Three..263
Chapter Fifty-Four 267
Chapter Fifty-Five 271
Chapter Fifty-Six..273
Chapter Fifty-Seven..275
Chapter Fifty-Eight 277
Epilogue 279
Acknowledgments 287
About the Author 289

PROLOGUE

My heart pounds and my hand shakes as I reluctantly open the door. Is he really gone? Tension overwhelms me. As I peek inside, I blink a couple of times because all I'm seeing is red. I shake my head and blink once more. I inhale the foul metallic odor coming from inside. I then realize what it is…it's blood, and it's everywhere. On the floor, on the walls, dripping like raindrops from the ceiling…I open my mouth to scream, but no sound comes out.

I awake with a start, gasping, and my eyes fly open. My heart is beating so fast and hard that it's painful. I take a deep breath and try to calm myself. "It's okay, Anna," I tell myself. "It's just a dream…a nightmare, one you've had many times before. Relax."

I take a deep breath and wonder…how does a person's whole life go by like the flutter of a butterfly's wing?

Lenore Sylvain Dexter

Lying here in my big bed in this darkened room, I try to catch my breath, reminding myself that I'm safe as I feel the softness of my own hand-sewn quilts wrapped around me like a cocoon.

I inhale and sigh. How frustrating it is that while my physical body is so weak and tired, my mind at this minute is as sharp as it's ever been. I know that I'm dying. The last blood test revealed that my major organs are starting to fail. The sad faces some of my family members wear when they visit me certainly don't help. I really don't want to be reminded that the end is near. I sigh once more, thinking I should be thankful for a full life after being on this earth for eighty-five years—and I am. There were a lot of positive events during those years, starting with good parents, a good husband, many children (twelve, as a matter of fact), and even more grandchildren, whom I truly treasure (forty-four at last count). I also have a few great-grandchildren, some of whom I've never met, as they live in different states. But as good as all those blessings are, there were a lot of dark years in my life as well. Lying here day after day with all this time on my hands, I can't help thinking about this life of mine, especially now that I know the end is near. I sigh yet again—it seems I've been doing a lot of that lately. I also talk aloud to myself more than I ever have. "I guess you need to thank God for the many blessings He gave you, old girl. Yeah, and while you're at it, you better ask Him to forgive you for the things you aren't so proud of and pray for absolution."

My granddaughter came to see me last week. She's my most frequent visitor, and I'm almost ashamed to admit she is my favorite. I know you aren't supposed to have favorite children or grandchildren. And while I never consciously favored any one of my children, she's different. Her name is also Anna, and I have to say that she has a very strong resemblance to me when I was her age. She is sixteen years old, and we've been close ever since she was born. Her father, Everett, and his family never strayed from West Langford. In fact, they only live two houses down. He married a very sweet girl named Maggie, and they blessed me with four wonderful grandchildren.

I remember it was last Tuesday. As was my usual pastime, I was in bed reading a novel—my favorite escape. There was a knock on my door.

"Come in."

"Hi, Grammy; how are you feeling today?" She didn't sound like her chipper self. I put the novel down.

"I'm fine, Anna. How was school?"

"Okay, I guess. I got a B on my history test, but I was hoping for an A. Our history teacher, Mrs. Blanchett, doesn't like giving As for some reason."

"Well, a B's not so bad...better than average!"

"I guess."

I knew by her tone of voice that something was up. "You seem kind of sad, Anna. Everything okay?"

She hesitated. "Grammy, I heard Mom and Dad talking last night. They say you don't have long to live. Can that be true?"

"Well, sweetie, I am an old woman." I smiled. "Everybody has to die sometime. I know it's hard to lose the people closest to you, but Anna, my love, that's life!"

"But I'm going to miss you so much. You've been a part of my life forever!" The tears in her eyes made my heart drop.

"Hey, I'll always be with you, my sweet, even after I die. Just look in your heart and I'll be there. You can talk to me anytime and maybe you won't actually hear *my* words, but I'll hear yours."

"It won't be the same."

"True, it won't, but I know you are a strong girl and you'll be fine."

Silently, she came to my bed, lay down beside me, and hugged me. I struggled not to cry…this sweet girl reminded me so much of myself when I was young and innocent. I made a snap decision. "Anna," I said, "If I ask you to do something for me, will you promise you won't tell anyone?"

"Of course, Grammy…what is it?"

"Well, I have something very personal I'd like to give you, BUT you have to promise me you won't go looking for it or read it until I'm gone. Can you do that? Can I trust you?"

"Yes, Grammy. I promise! What is it and where is it?"

"It's like a diary. I wrote it a long time ago. It's pretty much my life's story. I've never shared it with anyone, not even my own children. I'm thinking if I give it to you, you can read a page or two every night after I'm gone, and you'll feel just like I was right there with you."

She sat up and looked at me. "Wow, Grammy! I would be honored to have that treasure! Thank you!"

"Okay, then, my love. I'll tell you where to find it. If you go up in the attic toward the farthest wall in the front of the house, there's a trunk. And in that trunk, there's a satchel. If you open that up, you'll find it in there. There's a big black Bible with gold etching, but you'll also find a green book. But you *must* promise you won't go snooping until I'm gone. And once you read the whole thing, I want you to hide it. Maybe someday you can give it to your own granddaughter."

"You don't want Mom and Dad or any of the aunts and uncles to read it?"

"No, sweetie...just you. It'll be our special secret."

"Will it make me sad?"

"I don't know; I hope not. I'm hoping it will just make you feel closer to me."

"Cool! I love you so much, Grammy."

"I love you too, Anna, my girl."

*****

My Grammy Anna died a few weeks later, on August 12, 1970. Although my heart hurt thinking that I would never see or talk to my Grammy again, all during the wake and funeral I kept thinking about the diary and couldn't wait to get my hands on it. Finding it, I realized Grammy was right; it did help me feel closer to her. As much as I knew I was going to miss her in my life, I knew I'd always have a little piece of her in her writing and could be with her in spirit whenever I needed her. Throughout my lifetime, I would pick that journal up and read parts of it just to feel close to her. And eventually, I *did* share it with one of my granddaughters, Jayne. She was fascinated by it because she was so interested in our family history.

The satchel was exactly where Grammy said it would be. I did see the big black Bible and couldn't resist taking a look at it.

Lenore Sylvain Dexter

Grammy Anna's name was listed as Anna Roberts Fletcher. I'd heard rumors that she had been married before and that Aunt Evie and my dad had different fathers. According to the Bible, her first husband's name was Joseph Lee Fletcher. They had two children, Bernice and Evelyn. Grammy had told me a couple of years ago that her first child had died of scarlet fever when she was a young girl. Because I thought this must have been very sad for her, I didn't ask any questions. I hoped I would learn more once I started reading the diary.

When I took the Bible out, I immediately saw the green book. It was about the size of one of my schoolbooks. I slowly removed it, treating it with loving respect. After opening it, I recognized my Grammy's handwriting and sitting down on the attic floor, I began to read…

PART ONE

PART ONE

CHAPTER ONE

I was born and raised in a beautiful little town in Orange County, Vermont called West Langford. Some people would call it a kind of a backcountry hill town, but I, like most people who lived there, believed it was God's country. I didn't venture very far from it in all my years except maybe once, because all I needed or wanted was right there in that little town.

No matter what season it was, even as a young girl, I was amazed at the beauty of the land...the rolling green hills, the trout-filled brooks, and the clear blue skies in the summer. In contrast, winter looked like a wonderland, pure white and shimmery. Spring was always welcome after a cold winter. My sister, Ella, and I would get excited over the first crocus that popped out of the ground or the bright green buds that graced our many maple trees. The fall was the prettiest time of year; people from other places would drive through our town just to take in the vibrant colors that decorated the landscape. There was something about the smells of the air, both in the spring and in the fall. When the snow melted, the spring air was clean and pure, like the smell of bedsheets just off the line. Fall had its own smells, with the earthy bouquet of decaying leaves on the ground and the crisp aroma of freshly picked apples. It was a great place to grow up. My older siblings—brothers Lonny and Doug—and my sister Ella and I knew everyone in town, as they knew us. We were the Roberts family. Generations of our family lived in this town for years, and we were always well-respected.

People didn't lock their doors in the late 1800s. No need. West Langford was a safe haven for all ages. People normally valued each other and were always willing to help out a neighbor when need be. Most people who lived there worked farms, as we did, although there were men who worked other jobs in town, like the blacksmith, the undertaker, and the preacher. Some of the men worked in the bobbin mill or the sawmill. Of course, we had the few loggers who sold the logs to the sawmill. With the exception of schoolteachers—and we had only one—women took care of their families and homes. Children were also expected to help out with daily chores once they reached a certain age. Life was simple.

Papa had always known farming. He inherited our farm from Grampa Ev and Grammy Katherine. Grampa Ev built it himself in the mid-1800s. He even named it "The Hermitage." It was a beautiful white farmhouse with a wraparound porch and an attached barn. It was huge. Downstairs, we had a big country kitchen, a good-sized parlor, a sitting room, as well as Mama and Papa's bedroom. Off the kitchen was our mudroom, which led to the woodshed. At the end of the woodshed was our three-holer. At least we didn't have to go outside to get to the outhouse when nature called, as a lot of our neighbors did. I was glad for that, especially in the cold winters. I heard stories of neighbors visiting their outhouses at night only to be greeted by an unwelcome skunk!! The parlor was at the front of the house where we would sometimes entertain visitors, but mostly, our visiting was done at the kitchen table. There was an impressive staircase to the upstairs bedrooms. I remember Lonny and Doug getting in trouble for sliding down the banister when they were just young boys. Mama would yell, "One of these days one of you boys is gonna slip and fall and break your neck!" They would just laugh and run outside. Although there were five bedrooms upstairs, Papa used one for an office where he kept track of his farming books. Papa's office not only had his desk and office chair, but also a huge stuffed chair in the corner, and many a time when I was little, I used to curl up in it while Papa studied his books. It smelled of him and his pipe tobacco, and I was comforted by the smells…especially when Ella and I would spat, and I wanted to get away from her. I remember a very old photo of Grampa Ev and Grammy Katherine on the wall. Although I never met them because they died before I was born, I thought they looked like very unhappy, stern people. They looked scary. I asked Mama about them once and she told me that they were good people, good parents to Papa and his siblings, but they never showed their emotions. There weren't any hugs and kisses like I was used to getting. They seemed to take life a lot more seriously.

Papa had four brothers and five sisters. We grew up with many cousins, as most of Papa's family stayed in the area when they grew up and went out on their own. Because Papa was the oldest of the boys, the farm was offered to him when Grampa Ev decided he'd had enough of farming. Since it was pretty much Papa's whole life, he accepted. Mama told me there were some hard feelings with Papa's brother, Uncle Kenny, who was the second son. Uncle Kenny also wanted the farm, but because Papa was the firstborn and that's the way they did things back then, so it was to be. Uncle Kenny didn't speak to Papa for years. It wasn't until Grampa Ev's funeral that he came around and stopped holding the grudge.

Both Grampa Ev and Grammy Katherine lived with our family for the rest of their lives once Papa took over the farm. Only Lonny and Doug have faint recollections of them because at that time, they were pretty young.

Mama also came from a farming background. She was brought up in Woods River, the next town over. She had eight brothers and sisters, and she was also the oldest. Ella and I liked hearing her stories about how it was her responsibility to raise most of the younger kids when she was pretty much a kid herself. She had to make sure each brother or sister was assigned a daily chore, and if they didn't do it, she was the one who got in trouble. So, Mama not only had to do her own chores, but she had to check on them to make sure they had done theirs. She pretty much had kids around her all her life. One day when she was extra tired and fed up with yelling at the boys for their mischievousness, she exclaimed, "This is why I told your father I didn't want kids when he asked me to marry him." Once she saw the looks on our faces, she laughed and said she was just kidding. She said life just wouldn't be the same without us and she felt blessed that we were all hers.

She and Papa had met at a dance one summer night and were married by the fall. She said they just knew they were meant to be together, so why waste time? When I got older, I wondered if it was because she wanted to escape all the brothers and sisters she had to care for.

Mama made lots of clothes for her siblings and was a very good seamstress. She made all of our clothes, so she used one of the upstairs rooms for her sewing room. Ella would often retreat to that room when *she* needed a hideaway. Ella was always more interested in sewing and needlepoint than I was. Most days, I had a hard time sitting still. Besides, I just didn't have the patience to make all those tiny stitches that Mama said were so important.

Lonny and Doug, being the oldest, each had their own bedroom and Ella and I shared the largest of the five rooms. Our bedrooms were pretty simple because we really only used them to dress and sleep. We never went up there to play. We had a double bed and two dressers with mirrors hanging on the wall above them. There was also a very small closet to hold our dresses. We didn't have many of those, so one closet suited us just fine.

The barn attached to the house mostly contained Papa's farm tools. The only time I went into that barn was to get to the root cellar. When I was younger, I dreaded when Mama sent me to go down into that dank, dark place to fetch something she needed. It's where we stored the canned fruits, potatoes, carrots, and other vegetables. My brothers knew of my fear and sometimes would go on ahead of me and jump out at me when I was searching for what Mama wanted. I'd scream and cry and run back to Mama, and the boys would sometimes get a lashing, depending on Mama's mood, but she'd always hug me and comfort me and tell me not to cry. "Those brothers of yours can sometimes be so wicked," she'd tell me.

In the red barn, farther away from the house, we had cows, a couple of oxen to work the land, and a horse named Nellie. Nellie and I were friends. She was a workhorse, but gentle and friendly. I found that she was a great listener, too. Whenever I had something on my mind, I'd get the curry comb and brush her while I vented. Now that I look back at those vents, I think how unimportant and trivial they were. But when you're young, you tend to make mountains out of molehills.

Off the barn was a separate area where our pigs were, with access to an outdoor pen where they could do their favorite thing…root around in the mud. Our pigs were also friendly critters, but I tried not to get too attached to them because it might just happen that they would be our supper one evening. The chickens also had their own space, a coop that had to be cleaned on a regular basis. Ella hated our chickens. When she was younger and was feeding them one day, she slipped and fell and they all gathered around her, some pecking at her. She screamed like she was being murdered. Mama rescued her, but after that, she would sometimes bribe me to feed them when Papa asked her to do it. Of course, like all farms, we had many dogs and cats, who kept the rat and mouse population down in the barns. The dogs were all mutts, mostly given to us as puppies from other farmers when their dogs had litters. We had Duke and Sam and Buster and Grover. Papa wouldn't take a pup unless they were male. The cats didn't have names. They just kept reproducing and we couldn't even keep track of how many we had. They all lived in the barn or outside. We fed them all once a day and there was always water available for them. They seemed content to live with us.

Mama, Ella, and I always stayed busy with our many daily household chores as well as feeding the chickens and milking the cows when Papa and the boys weren't able to do it. Lonny and Doug helped Papa with the more physical chores, and there were many of those depending on the season. There was hardly an idle moment between helping with the animals and growing our gardens. Mama was a great cook, and Ella and I both loved helping her in the kitchen. Monday was laundry day, and it literally took all day using a wooden tub and washboard. Laundry was not my favorite thing to do. It was tedious and boring, but I did become pretty strong from lifting all the wet sheets week after week. All in all, life was good when I was young, the simple routine of living with my parents, siblings, and all our animals. I guess I never really stopped to realize just how good and simple life was at that time when I was such a young girl. I just took it for granted, but I think most children do. They don't overthink things like we tend to do as adults. They just accept whatever comes their way.

CHAPTER TWO

I remember the first time I saw him. I was in Sam Miller's store getting supplies on a warm summer day in July of 1904. Mama sent me out early in the morning to fetch flour, sugar, and a new bread pan, among other things. My reward was that I could pick out one of the sweets Sam sold at his counter, and Sam had a good variety. Papa had made me a cart when I was little, and now I used it to haul the supplies from the store. It had two wheels in the back and a larger one in the front. He attached a wooden handle so I could pull it along behind me, and he painted it red like the color of our barns. I have always loved my little cart, and when I was younger, I would load a litter of kittens in it and take them for a ride.

I liked going to the store. Sam was a nice old guy. He owned the place, but he sure didn't work too hard. If it was good weather, you would find him sitting on the store's porch smoking his pipe, watching the world go by. He had a dear, sweet wife named Freda, who pretty much waited on customers and did most of the work around the place. She was large for a woman, which Papa said was probably why Sam married her. She was able to do most of the physical labor in the store so Sam wouldn't have to. She never complained and seemed to be happy and content, so I guess it didn't bother her any that Sam was on the lazy side. They actually made a strange-looking couple when they were together, her being on the large side and Sam on the short, plump side. They had owned the store for years and because everyone in town went there, Sam was the one to go to hear all the town's gossip. Sam knew everything that went on in our little town. Mama said he was worse than an old woman.

For some reason, Sam wasn't sitting on the porch that day and Freda wasn't at the counter when I entered the store. While I was gathering the items Mama had on her list, I heard a man's deep, very strange-sounding voice. No one talked like *that* around here. He was asking Sam if he knew of any farms for sale, as he wanted to relocate here to this "pretty little town."

"Well, as a matter of fact," I heard Sam say, "Harold Smith just passed on a while ago, and his widow, Mary, is looking to sell. I can give you directions if you want to go check it out."

I got curious and very quietly took a peek around the sacks of flour. The stranger was very tall, very dark, and very thin. I was fascinated by the look of him because he sure didn't look like any of the big, burly farmers around here. His face was pleasant and smooth-looking, almost like he didn't spend much time outdoors. He wore a gray three-piece suit and an odd top hat to match. I had never seen anything like it. In his strange accented voice, he introduced himself as Joseph Fletcher, telling Sam he was from

Louisiana. I heard about Louisiana in school when we studied the states. I knew it was way down south and wondered about someone coming here from that far away. I figured he must have wanted to come here pretty badly because I imagined it would have been a long, uncomfortable ride by train or stagecoach.

The stranger said, "Thank you, sir. I sure would appreciate ya givin' me directions. You said the widow's name is Mary?"

"Yup," said Sam. "She really wants to go live with her sister in Massachusetts, so I'm sure she'd welcome your interest. Hang on a minute and I'll draw you a map. By the way, my name's Sam, and my wife, Freda, and I can pretty much getcha anything you might need if you decide to settle here. She had to go make a delivery to Mrs. Adams this morning. Poor old lady is crippled and can't get out by herself. We like to take care of our own around here."

"Whah, that's right nice," the stranger drawled and smiled. Sam was filling one of the candy jars he kept on the counter. Normally, my attention would be on the candy and which one I would choose today, but I couldn't help watching and listening to the two men.

"Yup, you'll find us friendly, all right. Anyway, I carry a full line of merchandise, from food to clothing to bear traps and saddles. And if I don't have it in the store, I can order it for you and get it here in no time. Plus, this here is the Post Office. I don't got telegraph service, though. You'd have to go to Bradford for that."

"Sure sounds handy ta me. Please, draw me that map to Mary's. I'm looking forward to meeting her and seeing her farm."

Well, it just so happened that Mary's farm was the next farm over from my parents' place, so without thinking, I popped around the corner and heard myself say, "I'll take him to Mary's." *Whoa! Was that me? Did I just offer to take a complete stranger to Mary's farm?* Both men looked at me, seemingly just as surprised as I felt.

Sam, with his jovial smile, laughed and said, "Well golly, Anna, I didn't even know you was in the store! But I guess it would make sense for you to show Mr. Fletcher the way." He glanced at Fletcher and announced, "Mr. Fletcher, this is Anna Roberts. She and her family live on the next farm over to Mary's. They're less than a mile apart."

Okay, I thought, *I guess if Sam thinks it's all right that I take him, then it must be okay.* I slowly walked toward the counter where the men were standing, still shocked at myself for making the offer. I was normally pretty shy, especially around strangers. Now, I was able to see his eyes better as he looked me over from head to toe. They were such dark eyes, so dark that I couldn't really determine the color…brown? Or could they be black? I'd never met anyone with black eyes. Anyway, the way he looked at me made me blush, and I looked away.

I was used to having friends who were boys. In fact, my best friend was Leo Decker, whom I'd known forever. He was a year younger than me. Leo was a cute kid with straight brown hair that was always too long and unruly. He was always pushing it out of his eyes. Many a time when I was with him, I wished I had a pair of scissors to chop off his locks. His eyes were crinkly and light brown with green flecks. Mama called them hazel. For the longest time, I was taller than he was—which wasn't very tall—but in the last year, he seemed to sprout up like a stalk of corn or a sunflower.

He and I grew up together, and I was closer to him than I was to my own siblings. We'd been going to school together ever since he was six and I was seven. In West Langford, we had one schoolhouse, and many grades were taught by the same teacher, Miss Everdeen Trumbull. Everyone loved Miss Everdeen. Some called her a spinster because she never married; therefore, she had no kids of her own. Rumor was that she had a beau, but he went away to war and got killed. She always referred to her students as her children, and she always treated us as such. Even when there were naughty kids who disrupted our studying, they were reprimanded with a stern kind of love. We were about thirty of us students in that one schoolroom, ranging in age from about six to fifteen. There was only the one large room with the teacher's desk in the front and smaller desks for us kids facing it. They were arranged in groups according to our ages. At the front of the room, behind the teacher's desk, was a big blackboard; on the side, there was a small closet where she kept supplies; and in the corner, a wood stove to keep us warm in the winter months. There were only two windows, and I'm pretty sure she set the classroom up with the windows at the back of the room so we wouldn't get distracted. It was a happy day when Miss Everdeen chose you to stay after and erase her perfectly formed letters on the board and clean the erasers at the end of the day. She gave that student extra attention as she chatted away and listened to us, wanting to know what was happening in our lives. Seems like all kids thrive on extra attention.

Leo and I walked to the schoolhouse together most days. In nice weather, it took us about a half hour, but we did have some brutal winters, and sometimes it would take over an hour. I remember one snowy day in January, it took us so long, slipping and sliding all the way. Once we got there, Jimmy Patterson, his sister, Lily, and Miss Everdeen were the only ones who made it. Jimmy and Lily only lived about five minutes away, so it wasn't surprising to see them. We waited for a while and when nobody else showed up, we were sent back home. I remember that it started snowing again as we were making our way back. I believe that snowstorm alone, during that harsh winter, left us with over two feet of snow. Mama sure seemed happy to see me when I walked back through the door that day. She didn't worry about us often, but that was a doozy of a storm with the wind and all. Mama called it a blizzard.

Yup, Leo and I were best buds and had been forever. When we were younger, many times Leo and I would take walks together to Woods River. We'd go fishing in the spring, make tree forts in the summer, and build snow caves in the winter. I liked having Leo as my best friend. He was funny and easy to be with. I think he probably felt at ease with me because he grew up with three older sisters and no brothers. His parents were older than Mama and Papa. I once heard Mama call Leo a mid-life baby…whatever that meant.

Although Leo was the one to blush when he looked at *me* lately, this feeling I was having as Mr. Fletcher's eyes were on me was new. All of a sudden, I felt very shy. Mr. Fletcher said, as his eyes locked onto mine, "Well, if y'all don't mind, Miss Anna, that would be very nice." He smiled and put his hands in his pockets. I noticed dimples in his cheeks. "Why don't you settle with Sam here while I load your supplies into my buggy. I'll help you get them home before we head out to Mary's farm."

Sam sold a lot of his merchandise on credit because most of us didn't have cash on a regular basis. When Papa sold a hog or a cow, we would be able to clear up our debt with Sam, and most neighbors did the same. I stuttered, "A—all right, then, but my cart is outside to haul the supplies home. Can I leave it here, Sam, for a bit, so I can introduce him to Mama and Papa first before we go to Mary's? I'll come by and pick it up later if that's okay."

"Of course, Anna," replied Sam. Turning to Mr. Fletcher, he said, "Hope to be seeing ya around our little town soon, Mr. Fletcher." I couldn't help but notice that Sam had a piece of blue lint on his lip, and it moved up and down as he spoke. I wondered if I should tell him about it, but I didn't want to embarrass him in front of the stranger, so I kept quiet.

Mr. Fletcher replied, "Thank you, Sam…I hope so, too." My eyes followed him as he walked out the door.

He was already in the driver's seat when I came out. Climbing into the seat next to him, I felt pretty nervous. Off we went…me looking anywhere but at him, and him seeming unable to take his eyes off me. I was wishing I had worn my bonnet that day so I could hide my face. He had a pretty fancy buggy compared to Papa's, and the seats were soft and smooth. I couldn't help but run my fingers over the soft leather. He told me his horse was named Blaze and that he'd bought him and the buggy from a horse farm in Benton. I admired Blaze and told him so. "Blaze struts like he's a proud horse," I said. Mr. Fletcher looked at me with arched eyebrows and smiled. All of a sudden, for some reason, I remembered that in all the excitement, I had forgotten the sweet that was promised me at Sam's store—but that didn't seem very important to me right now.

I was happy he had a horse and buggy, and the ride was considerably quicker than if we had to walk. It was a beautiful morning with a slight breeze that felt very refreshing; I was glad for it since I was feeling a little flush. The trees along the dusty dirt road were tall and lush, and as I listened to the steady *clip-clop* of the horse's hooves, I stared at the shadows the trees made across the road and wondered about this strange man. As I was deep in thought, he suddenly asked me how old I was, which I considered strange, because at the same time I was wondering how old *he* was. To me, it seemed he had a mature man's face on a young man's body, so it was hard to tell. Of course, I would never have the nerve to ask him his age, so I told him I was fourteen, but in the fall I would be fifteen. He told me I was a "pretty lil' thing." That made me blush all over again, and I looked down into my lap.

Sometimes when I got nervous, I would fiddle with my fingers. Noticing that I was doing that now, I made a conscious effort to stop. It wasn't every day that a perfect stranger told me I was pretty. Oh, Mama and Papa sometimes made comments like, "We gotta watch our little girl…she's starting to turn heads!" Sometimes Ella would look at me like I did something to make her mad, and then there was Leo, whom I would catch staring at me from time to time like he was looking at the biggest trout in the brook! I guess I figured out that I wasn't bad to look at. Looks were never important to me, so I never gave it much thought, although it did make me feel very special right about then.

CHAPTER THREE

Once we got to our farm and drove up into the yard, he exclaimed, "Wow! This place is beautiful. Looks just like the picture I saw in a book I read when I was learning about Vermont farming."

I'd always been proud of our farm. I knew our farm was bigger than most of the neighboring farms, and Grampa Ev's house *was* pretty impressive. We both got out of the buggy and he followed me, carrying the supplies into the kitchen. Mama and Ella were standing at the table canning green beans. Mid-summer was the time we had to can all our garden vegetables, which included not only beans but all kinds of vegetables…tomatoes, carrots, squash, and cucumbers. Cucumbers meant pickles to me. I loved Mama's pickles! She made mustard pickles and tongue pickles, and my favorite…bread and butter pickles. She looked up in surprise back and forth between the two of us and asked, "Anna?" I said, "Hi Mama." I started taking the supplies out of Mr. Fletcher's hands and placing them on the counter as I said, "This here is Mr. Fletcher. He's interested in buying Mary's farm, so I'm going to take him on over to meet her." Everyone knew Mary couldn't wait to start a new life in Massachusetts.

Relieved of his packages, Mr. Fletcher removed his hat and extended his hand, saying, "Ma'am, pleased to meet ya."

When Ella turned to look at him, she was quick to wipe her hands on her apron, take it off, and offer her hand. She said, smiling, "Hello, Mr. Fletcher. I'm Ella Roberts, Anna's older sister."

"Well, hello, Miss Ella; nice to meet you." Then he addressed Mama. "Ma'am...y'all have a beautiful place here. I was telling Anna that it looks just like a picture I saw in a book back in Louisiana."

"Why, thank you, Mr. Fletcher. We like it. You're from Louisiana?"

"Yes, ma'am...a long way away, I know, but I'm hoping to settle here in Vermont, and if all works out, I'll be your neighbor."

Now, like I said, West Langford was a safe haven, so I never really had any reason to fear anybody. But the look on Mama's face made me feel a little uncomfortable, like when that stray dog wandered into our yard. She looked again from me to Mr. Fletcher and said, "Anna, you know what? Leo's in the cow barn with Papa and the boys right now. Why don't you go introduce Mr. Fletcher and ask Leo to go on with the two of you to Mary's."

"Leo's here? How come?" Leo only came this early when school was in session. He had many chores to do on his own farm.

Mama smiled and said, "I think he was waiting on *you* to get home."

"Oh, okay," I said, puzzled. "Sure, I'll ask him."

Mr. Fletcher bowed slightly to Mama and Ella and said, "Again, nice to meet both you fine ladies. I'm sure I'll be seeing more of y'all if I buy the farm."

Mama smiled. "Good luck! I know Mary's itching to leave, so you probably have a good chance of getting it." I gave Mama a peck on the cheek, glanced at Ella's starry eyes, rolled my eyes, and motioned for Mr. Fletcher to follow me.

Walking to the barn, Mr. Fletcher looked down at me and asked if I had any other siblings. He was still holding his hat, and I noticed his hair was wavy and a very dark brown. I told him I had two older brothers named Lonny and Doug. Lonny was almost twenty-one and Doug was twenty. Lonny and Doug looked nothing alike, kinda like me and Ella. Lonny favored Papa with his black hair and blue eyes, while Doug was fair and looked more like Mama and me. They were both tall, and in my opinion, very handsome. Lonny was strong-willed, stubborn, and determined, while Doug was mild-mannered, kind, and thoughtful. I loved them both—more so now that they were older and didn't pick on me as much. Many a single girl in West Langford and surrounding towns had their eyes on my brothers, but like some farmers, the farm took up all their time and energy, so seeking a wife was not on the top of their list. What I didn't tell Mr. Fletcher was that after Mama had Doug, she had a few miscarriages. No one ever talked about it, but Papa had told me about it once and said it was a very sad time for Mama.

Once we entered the barn, some of my favorite smells surrounded me…animals, sawdust, and hay. These were the smells I grew up with, and they meant home. I saw Papa, Lonny, Doug, and Leo bent down examining Molly, our best milker. We had about five milkers, two calves, and a bull. The calves were born in the spring, but it was customary to butcher at least one of them in the fall for meat. That was always difficult for me. Papa mostly kept the bull in the pasture and warned me to steer clear of him 'cause he tended to have a mean streak. That was fine with me. Ol' Charlie was big and strong and always scared me.

"Is something wrong with Molly, Papa?" I asked when I saw how intent the four of them seemed to be, hovering around the cow.

Not bothering to look up, Papa said, "Looks like poor Molly has some kind of infection on her udder, Anna. I'm thinking we may have to ask Doc Hayes to come have a look at her." Forgetting all about Mr. Fletcher, I immediately walked over to her and rubbed her soft pink nose. I always thought that cows had the best eyes. They were big and brown, and they looked at you with love. I glanced up and noticed Leo staring at our newcomer, Mr. Fletcher.

"She'll be ok, honey," Papa said soothingly. He knew how attached I was to all our animals, except maybe Charlie. That's why I had a hard time with the butchering of our calves. Looking back at Leo, he said, "Right, son?" Papa knew that Leo was probably just as concerned about Molly as I was. Seeing Leo staring in a different direction, he turned around to see why the boy looked so dumbfounded. Papa stood up and said, "Oh; sorry, mister. Didn't know you was here!" Now, all eyes were on Mr. Fletcher.

Embarrassed, I rattled off, "I'm sorry, Papa; this here is Mr. Joseph Fletcher from Louisiana, hoping to buy Mary Smith's farm. He thinks West Langford is a pretty town and wants to settle here." Mr. Fletcher looked at me with amusement, as he probably realized I was listening in on the whole conversation between him and Sam.

Looking back toward my father, he said, "Hello, sir; nice to meet y'all. Call me Joe." He shook Papa's hand.

"Well, welcome, Joe. My name's Elmer Roberts. These are my boys, Lonny and Doug, and this here is Anna's friend, Leo Decker. How is it that you two are acquainted?" Papa asked, confused, looking back and forth between the two of us just like Mama had.

I spoke up. "I met him at Sam's store. When I heard he was interested in seeing Mary's farm, I offered to take him."

"It was quite neighborly of Anna to offer," Mr. Fletcher said, smiling at me. He turned and nodded a hello to the boys.

Papa continued, "Louisiana, huh? That's quite a ways from Vermont. What brings you here?" Now I was all ears, and instead of Leo looking at Mr. Fletcher, he was staring at me!

"Well," said Joe, "I decided I wanted to experience a simpler life. Farming here in Vermont appealed to me, and while I have to admit I don't know all that much about it yet, I figured I could hire out some farmhands to help me learn the business."

Papa smiled his mischievous smile and said, "Well, son, farming ain't no easy business. Takes a lot of hard work from sunup to sundown. You definitely need a good, experienced farmhand *and* a good woman to take care of you while you're taking care of the farm." I loved that Papa appreciated Mama. "You got a wife and kids coming with you?"

"No, sir," Joe replied, hanging his head. "My wife died giving birth to our first child, and the baby died a few days later. I never did remarry. That was about two years ago," he continued sadly. Then he glanced over at me. I blushed as I noticed Leo was staring at me again, and he was turning a bright shade of red himself.

"Well," said Papa, "I'm sorry to hear that, son. Maybe you'll find a bride here in West Langford. We grow our girls strong and hardy." Papa chuckled. By that time, I think my face matched the color of Leo's, and I put *my* head down.

After a second, though, I looked up at Leo and said, "Leo…wanna come with us to Mary's? Mama said you'd probably want to go with me."

Leo looked with hope at my father, and of course, Papa nodded. "Sure, go with Anna and Joe, and maybe you and Anna can go a little farther to the Doc's house and ask him to come take a look at Molly when he gets a chance."

"Sure thing, Mr. Roberts," Leo replied happily. Leo totally respected my father and would do anything for him.

CHAPTER FOUR

The ride to Mary's in Mr. Fletcher's buggy took less than ten minutes. We were all silent as we rode along the bumpy road, swaying back and forth, with me in the middle trying hard not to crash into this tall, dark stranger. I was trying not to fiddle with my fingers as I wondered whether I was the only one who felt uncomfortable. We were all so silent. It made me feel weird and uncomfortable that both Mr. Fletcher and Leo kept stealing glances at me.

Mary's farm was quite a bit smaller than ours. She and Harold had some milking cows, some hogs and chickens, but not as many animals as we had. Once Harold got sick, Mary had to sell off some of her livestock so she could support herself and her children. When we pulled into Mary's land, a couple of mangy mutts bounded toward us, barking up a storm. Leo got out first and greeted the pups as they jumped up and licked his face. Leo had always been good with animals—he loved them and they loved him. This was apparently not the case with Mr. Fletcher. When he got down from the buggy, one of the dogs started growling at him, but Leo reprimanded it and the dogs ran on ahead. I heard Mr. Fletcher mutter something under his breath that didn't sound very nice, but I couldn't hear what it was. I wondered if he had a problem with animals. Some men did. I used to hear horror stories about how some mean men would abuse their animals. I was hoping Mr. Fletcher didn't have *that* cruel side to him.

We found Mary in her lush garden, picking tomatoes. Her three little children were running up and down the rows, laughing and playing. They stopped suddenly when they saw us walking toward them. The oldest, Kara, yelled, "It's Anna! Hi, Anna! And Leo's here, too!!" All of them scooted up to me for hugs. Kara was seven, Dean was five, and little Harold was only three. While Mary's husband was in the hospital, I would often babysit the kids so she could go visit him. Harold was only thirty-five years old when he got pneumonia. Seemed like every year someone would die from that dreaded ailment. That was the first funeral I had ever attended, and I thought to myself that I never wanted to go to another funeral again. Everyone cried and carried on so. And even though I didn't know Harold all that well, I found myself sobbing as they lowered him into the rich Vermont soil.

Mary stood up and stretched, looking very strained and tired. Mary was Lonny's age but looked much older. They had gone to school together, and I always thought she had an eye for him. Not to be mean, but Mary was quite homely and plain. She was so thin, she looked like one of Mama's green beans. Her eyes looked like they were a bit too small for her face while her mouth looked like it was a tad too big. But Mary was a sweetheart and didn't have a mean bone in her body. She was wearing an old calico dress that looked like it had seen better years and a huge, bright-yellow sun bonnet along with a full-length apron that was dirty and ragged. "Hello, Anna; hello, Leo. What brings you here?"

"Well," I said, "Mary, this is Mr. Joe Fletcher. He wants to settle here and was asking about your farm."

That brought a smile to Mary's wide mouth. She dusted off her hands and extended one to him. "Nice to meet you, Mr. Fletcher. Are you really serious about buying a place here in West Langford?"

"Call me Joe, ma'am, and yes I am. Anna was kind enough to show me the way here after Sam Miller told me y'all wanted to sell. I'm sorry to hear about your husband. I'm sure it must be very difficult for you and your children."

Tears sprang to Mary's eyes and she looked down at her stained hands. "Thank you. That's kind of you to say. If Anna and Leo don't mind watching the kids, I'll show you around the farm now if you want."

Joe replied, "I'd like that, Mary." They both looked at us expectantly.

Leo and I looked at each other and simultaneously replied, "Okay."

Leo and I picked up where Mary left off gathering vegetables, and Leo made a game out of it for the kids, saying, "Whoever picks the most tomatoes wins!! And remember, only pick the RED ones!" Giggling, the kids pitched in, filling baskets with the ripe, red orbs, occasionally biting into the juicy fruit and staining their clothes with the bright-red juice.

By the time Mary and Mr. Fletcher came back around an hour later, we were all sitting on the grass. I watched as Leo played with the kids, letting them climb all over him while ear-splitting shrieks of joy filled the air. The dogs were running and barking all around them, excited by the play. When I looked up to see Mary, she wore a huge smile and looked years younger. "Looks like you're going to have a new neighbor, you two!" she beamed. "Now me and the kids can go live with my sister in Massachusetts. I think life will be much better for us."

"That's great, Mary!" And to Mr. Fletcher, I said, "And welcome to West Langford, Mr. Fletcher." Leo got up and stood silently while the kids pulled on him, still carrying on. I thought he looked as though he were sulking.

"You know, Anna, you can call me Joe. Please."

"Okay, *Joe*," I said slowly, testing it out. I looked at Mary. "Well, Leo and I have to run along to see Doc Hayes. Our cow, Molly, needs his help."

"All right, then," said Mary. "Thanks for bringing Joe around. Be sure to tell your Mama and Papa 'hey' for me. And thanks for watching these *rowdy* kids," she continued, emphasizing *rowdy* as she looked accusingly at Leo.

Leo smiled sheepishly. As we were saying our good-byes, Joe said, "Anna, can I talk to you alone for a minute?" That caught me off guard. I glanced at Leo and saw the surprise in his eyes, so I quickly looked away.

"Umm...sure." He took me by the elbow over a ways, and I could feel Leo's eyes boring through me. I was glad the kids were trying to distract him.

"Anna," he said, "If it's okay with you, I'd like to come to your house tonight. Talk to your father about farming and all...would that be all right with you?"

*Why is he asking **my** permission?* I wondered. I replied, "I guess so. I'll let Mama know, and I'm sure they'd want you to come for supper."

"Well, that would be very kind. I'd like that very much." To my surprise, he took both my hands in his, looked into my eyes, and said, "See you tonight, Anna."

On the way to Doc's place, Leo was unusually quiet. I guess I was still thinking about Joe's question and the way he was looking at me, so I was being pretty quiet myself. I was also hoping Leo didn't see the hand-holding.

"What do you think about that Joe guy, Anna?" Leo was kicking rocks.

"What do you mean, what do I think of him?"

"You know, do you 'like' him?"

"Sure," I said, "he's all right."

"I mean do you *like* him? Because I sure do think he likes you!"

"Really?" I asked innocently.

"He just looked at you like he wanted to eat you up!" exclaimed Leo.

"Oh, come on, Leo...he did not."

"Well, *I* sure don't like him. Why did he want to talk to you alone? What did he want?"

"See," I said, "You're just being silly. All he wanted to know was if he could come by tonight and talk to Papa about farming."

"Did I see him holding your hands?"

"Oh, Leo, he was just being nice. He's from the South. They probably do that all the time in Louisiana."

"Well, just be careful around him, that's all. He's old."

Rolling my eyes, I said, "Sure, Leo; I will."

CHAPTER FIVE

Doc Hayes and his wife, Grace, lived in a small farmhouse a ways back from the main road. They had a brood of kids, but they all grew up and moved away. I wasn't very good at guessing ages, but I'd say Doc and Grace were pretty old...both around seventy. The Doc had been looking after our animals ever since I could remember. Papa said he was the best and West Langford was lucky to have him. He always had a gentle way about him, and I guessed the animals sensed it, too. Grace opened the door when we knocked. "Why, hello, Anna, Leo...is this a social visit?" When we were little, we would visit Grace sometimes because she made the best cookies, and her cookie jar was full all the time. She always welcomed us.

"Hi, Mrs. Hayes. No, 'fraid not. Papa sent us over because our cow Molly needs the Doc."

"Oh, sorry to hear about Molly, Anna. The Doc is over at the Jameses' farm right now. One of their mares is foaling, but when he gets home, I'll be sure to let him know. In the meantime, you two have time for some milk and cookies?"

Leo and I looked at each other, and I could see that Leo was thinking what I was thinking. "Sure, Mrs. Hayes! Thanks!"

Their home was so inviting—everything from the comfortable kitchen chairs to the warm colors that graced their walls. I sometimes wondered if Mrs. Hayes was lonely for her children. Why they would all want to move away from here was a mystery to me. I decided to be bold that day and I asked, "Why are all your children so far away?"

"Oh…well, Anna, they apparently got their father's brains because all of them pursued educations in animal husbandry. The jobs they found took them all over New England. Matthew and Nathan are in Connecticut; James is in Massachusetts; Loraine is the farthest away…in Baltimore, of all places… working for the government! Eva is also in Massachusetts; George and Carol are in New Hampshire; Gerard and little Donald are in Maine. Although not so little anymore. Ha! It's always that way with the baby of the family." She smiled. "They are all very educated and respected in their fields. Doc and I are very proud of all of them. When you're a parent, sometimes you just have to let go and let your children live their own lives. They always come for the holidays, and those times are always very special to us. We have fifteen and a half grandchildren now." She laughed. "Gerard's wife, Ann, is about five months along. Know this, my young friends: if you grow old and see that the children you brought into this world turn out to be good, God-fearing, responsible adults, you've done your part in the world."

CHAPTER SIX

That evening, Joe showed up, looking quite handsome and nothing like a farmer. He wore a similar suit to the one I saw him wearing at Sam's store. This time, though, he didn't have a top hat. The suit was a dark brown, like the color of his eyes. Since he was wearing a change of clothes, I wondered where he was staying. He knocked, and Ella answered the door. We were all sitting at the table visiting and anticipating Mama's meal. "Come in, Mr. Fletcher. Supper's almost ready," she announced with a welcoming smile.

He walked through the door without even a glance at Ella and exclaimed, "Mmm...something smells wonderful! My mouth's watering."

Mama answered, "Why, thank you, Joe. We're glad to have you join us tonight. It's nice to see you again." Lowering her voice, she added, "Elmer told me about your wife and child. I'm very sorry for you. To lose both your wife and your child…well, I can't even imagine. I do know a little about what it's like to lose a child, and I know it can be devastating." Ella and I looked at each other in shock. Mama had NEVER mentioned her miscarriages before.

"Thank you, Mrs. Roberts. I appreciate your concern," Joe replied somberly.

Mama nodded at him and said, "But on a happier note, Anna said you and Mary came to an agreement on her farm. I guess congratulations are in order!"

"Yup, I'm pretty happy about it. Can't wait to get farmin'!!" The boys thought Joe's comment was funny and started laughing. It was infectious and we all joined in. Papa was already sitting at the table anticipating his meal. When he heard Mama's comment about congratulations, Papa raised his cider cup like he was toasting and took a swallow. I think I was the only one who noticed, and I smiled. After a very hard, long day of working, Papa did enjoy his cider! He often sat at the table and visited with us girls while we cooked and the boys finished up for the day. The kitchen table was definitely our visiting place. I often wondered why Grampa Ev had even bothered with a parlor.

Mama was making chicken pot pie for supper, and Joe was right—the kitchen smelled so good it made your stomach growl. Papa got up from the table and said, "Come on, Joe; we got a few minutes before dinner's ready. The boys and I'll show you around the farm while the girls finish up here." Because it was summer, the days were long and it wasn't quite dark yet.

When it was time to eat, Ella volunteered to go find the men. I knew Ella was very interested in our dinner guest. Right after I

Sugarhouse Trials

announced that Joe would be coming for dinner, I saw her dash upstairs. She wore her best blue Sunday dress and the brooch Mama and Papa had given her for her sixteenth birthday. I thought she looked very pretty and wondered what Joe thought of her. Of course, Mama outdid herself with her cooking, and the meal tasted even better than it smelled. Everyone knew Mama was one of the best cooks in West Langford. She loved being in the kitchen, and I was glad she was teaching Ella and me all her secrets and sharing her own Mama's recipes with us. Mama always said, "The way to a man's heart is through his stomach."

Dinner conversation was mostly about farming. Joe had many questions, and Papa had all the answers. Lonny and Doug contributed, too, seeing they had been farming since they were toddlers. Mostly, Mama, Ella, and I just sat quietly and listened, and I noticed that Ella hardly took her eyes off Joe.

While we were all enjoying the tart apple pie Mama made for dessert, Joe said to Papa, "I guess you got *yourself* a mighty fine wife here, Elmer." His eyes widened. "You're sure a lucky man to be able to eat like *this* every day! Someday I hope to be as lucky." Then he glanced quickly at *me!* I'm pretty sure Ella and I were the only ones who noticed, and I looked down at my pie. I thought, *Why didn't he look at Ella just then?* Everybody else laughed, and I didn't dare look back at Ella. I could tell Joe felt quite at home here and really liked our family. And they all seemed to like him, too.

After we ate, as we continued to sit around the table, Joe asked Papa some more questions about farmhands and livestock. He said he was thinking of buying some sheep to go along with the livestock Mary was selling with the farm. Papa said that was a really good idea and told Joe about a couple of farms around the area where he could buy quality animals. Papa also mentioned that he knew of a hardworking farmhand named Buddy Patterson that was always looking for work. "Buddy's a friend of mine and can teach you all you need to know. He'd been farming for years but decided to quit farming for himself. Now he works for other farmers who need *his* help. In fact, he had a herd of sheep himself at one time, so he'd even be a help to you there."

"What kind of name is Buddy, Elmer? Did his father really name him Buddy?"

Papa laughed. "No, Joe. His given name is Earl. His father's name was also Earl, so they gave Buddy the nickname so there'd be no confusion."

"Wow!" I exclaimed. "I never knew that! I always thought his name was just Buddy!" Everyone chuckled.

Buddy and Papa were great friends, and Buddy often came to visit and have supper with us because Papa welcomed his advice on farming problems. Grizzly-faced Buddy was like family, and we all liked him very much. He had a modest house over by the bobbin mill and lived with his sister, Cora. I often wondered why neither of them ever married. I knew they lost their parents at a very early age, and I guessed that they just decided to stay single and take care of each other. Buddy taught Lonny and Doug how to shoot a rifle, and many a time he'd take the boys hunting for deer, turkeys, or rabbits. My brothers idolized him, and they were like sons to him.

"Well, he sounds like just the person I'm looking for," said Joe. "When can I meet him?"

"I'll take you over tomorrow if you want," Papa offered as he lit his pipe.

"Sounds good, but it'll have to be later next week because I have to go to Bradford and make arrangements to get the sale of the farm going. As y'all know, Mary's in a hurry to get out and off to Massachusetts to be with her sister, and I'm looking forward to having my own home and be sleeping in my own bed."

"No problem," Papa answered. "Just come around when you're ready. Where ya been staying, anyway?" Papa refilled his cider cup. He offered Joe a cup, but Joe refused.

"I'll take some more of your iced tea, though, Mrs. Roberts." It was almost comical the way Ella scooted out of her chair to refill his glass. "Actually, I'm staying in East Kent at Mabel Paige's boarding house. It's a nice enough place and Mabel is very hospitable. She makes good pies, and don't y'all repeat this, but they can't compare to yours, Mrs. Roberts."

Mama kinda blushed, which was very unusual for her, and said, "I know Mabel. I go to her sewing circle sometimes. She is a friendly and kind person." I knew Mabel, too. She was a typical grandmother type...round as she was tall, with apple cheeks and always wearing a smile.

The clock struck nine, and Ella coyly asked Joe if he'd like another piece of Mama's pie. She also mentioned that she helped bake it, but he declined as he held his stomach, saying if he ate another bite of anything he'd burst. It got kind of quiet all of a sudden and then Joe asked, "Elmer, would it be all right if Anna took a little walk with me outside? It's such a beautiful night."

Our family must have looked quite silly as all our eyes got big in surprise. Mama stared at Papa as he said, staring back at Mama, "That's fine, but not for too long. Anna's got to tend to her chores early tomorrow morning."

Usually, I got up at 5:00 a.m. During school season, I had to be ready when Leo came by at 7:30. This was a busy time for Papa and the boys, so Ella and I took turns with the milking and chickens. One day I'd feed the chickens while she milked the cows, and the next day we'd switch. Papa would feed the animals while the boys were busy mucking out the stalls and shoveling the manure. Tomorrow was my morning to milk the cows. Because it took less time to feed the chickens and collect the eggs, we'd always help each other with the milking, even though Ella would rather go inside to help Mama. Sometimes I told her to just go help Mama. I liked kitchen work, but I really enjoyed spending time in the barn with the animals. Immediately I looked down, trying to hide my red face. Ella huffed, left the table, and headed upstairs. I hoped Mr. Fletcher hadn't noticed her rudeness, but he seemed totally oblivious to Ella's feelings. Mama started gathering the dirty dishes and didn't even yell to Ella to get back and help. Papa told the boys to say good night, so they did, and then Papa looked at me and said again as he got up from the table… "Don't stay out too long, now. Joe, I'll see you soon. Good luck in Bradford."

Standing and addressing both Mama and Papa, Joe said, "Thank you for the delicious supper. Mrs. Roberts, that was one of the best meals I've ever eaten. I'm truly obliged. Good night, Elmer, and thanks for your help. Good night, y'all."

Well, by now, my heart was in my throat. I hoped he couldn't see my hands shaking as I draped my shawl over my shoulders. Why did he want to take a walk with *me*? I wondered what Mama and Papa were thinking.

As Joe said, the evening was beautiful. The air smelled of newly cut grass and farm animals. It was a clear night, and the moon was full and silvery blue as it lit the yard. I could see the shadows of the maple trees that lined our drive, standing like sentries as if they were guarding our property. As we walked toward the cow barn, a dog barked in the distance, which made our dogs start up. "Hush," I hissed and was surprised that they actually listened to me. A nightingale called out as the butterflies went crazy in my stomach. Joe reached out and held my hand as we made a bit of small talk. I got a little chill, even though it was July.

"Anna, I know you said you were only fourteen, and I've only known you for a day, but I'd really like to get to know you better," he said, squeezing my hand as he spoke the word "better."

Whoa! I really didn't see that coming. We stopped. I turned and looked up into his dark eyes, which I had realized earlier were a very deep shade of brown, and said timidly, "Okay." He turned back in the direction of our house, smiled big, and told me I'd better scoot back home before Elmer came after him with his rifle...but not before kissing me on the cheek! Barely sane, I said, "Good night, Joe."

And he said, "I'll see y'all real soon, Anna, and hopefully every single day of my life after that."

A teenage girl doesn't know the meaning of infatuation. I was pretty much convinced that the feelings I was having was "love." I had never felt like this EVER before, so it must be love, I figured. I had a hard time falling asleep that night thinking how much life could change in only one day. I didn't know if Ella was asleep, but I was glad she was quiet so I could think. It was as if I'd gone from being a little girl when I woke up this morning, looking forward to the sweet I was going to get at Sam's store, to that night being a woman who was about to be courted by a handsome Southern gentleman. As I pulled the covers over my shoulders and put my hand on the cheek he kissed, I thought about this most unusual day, going over every detail until my eyes finally closed and I fell asleep.

CHAPTER SEVEN

The next several days went by the same as always, feeding the chickens, milking the cows, helping Mama in the kitchen, and mending clothes. For a couple of days, I met Leo at Mary's place to help her pack. I couldn't believe the change in Mary. No longer did she look like a sour, tired woman older than her age. "As much as I miss Harold with all my heart," she confessed, "I'm not gonna miss the farm and all the work that goes with it." Mary was folding the children's winter clothes and packing them neatly into one of the many wooden crates we got from Sam's store. "West Langford has always been my home…it's gonna be strange living with my sister in Massachusetts, but she needs my help right now and I need hers, so hopefully, it will work out just fine." I could tell she was excited about her new adventure, but I also heard some uneasiness in her voice. I understood it was kind of scary not knowing what to expect about the future. I sorta felt the same about Joe wanting to be in my life.

"Is your sister married?" I asked, picking through clothes.

"Engaged. Doris and her fiancé are planning to get married in a couple of years. Her future husband, Henry, is a practical, educated man who works at a bank. Doris told me he wants to save up some money first so he can buy them a house to live in before they marry and have children."

"Where does she live now?" asked Leo as he was busy packing Mary's linens in an old trunk Mama gave her.

"Up until she heard I was coming, she was living in a tenement working at a local factory, but she wasn't very happy in the tenement or at the factory. The tenement had a couple of small rooms, and she lived with three other women. One of them had a baby, so she didn't get much peace. She recently found another place to rent closer to Henry's bank where the kids and I can stay with her until she moves in with Henry."

I doubt she's going to find any peace with Mary's three kids, I thought as she spoke, but I would never say something rude like that out loud.

Mary continued, "Doris said Henry was able to get her a part-time job at his bank that could turn into a full-time job in the future. With her bank salary, the money I have from Harold, and the sale of the farm, she was able to find us a decent place where we'll all be comfortable."

"Well," I said, "It sounds like a good life. I can see why you're excited to go."

One of my jobs that day was looking out the window, watching the kids play outside to make sure they weren't doing anything they weren't supposed to do. So far, so good. They were playing hide

Sugarhouse Trials

and seek. One kid turned away while the other two hid. As they took turns hiding, I almost wished I was outside playing with them. It looked like a lot of fun. But my other job was sorting the winter clothes from the summer clothes so Mary would have an easier job of unpacking the necessities once she got there.

"I *am* excited, Anna. I'm hoping that maybe I can get a part-time job at one of the factories when the kids are in school, too, because once Doris moves out, the rent will all be on me."

"Can I ask where your parents are?" Leo asked hesitantly.

"Of course," Mary replied and smiled. "Ma and Pa left years ago for Canada. My ma's parents lived there and needed help once they got older. It was right after Harold and I got married. Doris didn't want to go…she's younger than me…in fact, she's the baby of the family. All my other ten siblings are scattered throughout Vermont. Doris and I, being the youngest, were closer to each other than the rest. Anyway, when Doris heard about my mother's aunt, Great-Aunt Marie in Massachusetts, and how she was getting on in years, Doris offered to go live with her in her cold flat. My aunt was overjoyed and welcomed her. Once Aunt Marie passed on, Doris decided she liked Massachusetts and went to live in the tenement."

I couldn't help but ask, "Didn't your great-aunt have any children of her own?"

"No; unfortunately, she and my Great-Uncle Martin tried to have kids, but it wasn't meant to be. Don't know much else about it."

As I watched the kids play, I thought about how very different people's lives can be. I liked hearing people's stories. Everyone had one.

CHAPTER EIGHT

That first day we were with Mary, we got everything packed in crates and trunks; the second day, we loaded up her old green wagon. Leo did most of the loading with my help. Her wagon was full as Leo hitched it to the horse. He thought it would be a good idea to take the horse for a little ride to get him used to the load he'd be carrying. Papa convinced Mary to buy a younger horse to make the trip south. He also offered to take Mary and the children all the way, but Mary refused.

"You are so very kind, Elmer, but I know you got your own farm to run. I'm not gonna take you away from that and your family. The roads are good, and so is the weather. It's not that far over the border. I'm sure I can get me and my brood safe and sound to our destination, but thank you. Couldn't have asked for better neighbors and friends than you and your family." As it turned out, Buddy went with Mary. Both he and Papa couldn't see her making that trip alone with three kids, and Buddy was happy to do it. Once he got back, he'd be working with Joe.

Mary was planning to leave in two days, so after we took the horse, wagon, and kids for a little ride, Leo brought it back to the barn and unhitched the horse. We wished Mary a safe trip and said our good-byes, and then we went to find the kids one last time. They hugged me and jumped on Leo. There were no sad good-byes with these three, and I was glad of it. I was going to miss these kids that I grew so attached to, and so was Leo. "We'd make some pretty fine parents someday, wouldn't we, Anna?"

I hesitated a minute because at first, I thought he meant us as a couple and it startled me. But then I realized he didn't mean it like that, so I said, "Time will tell, Leo…but I hope so."

CHAPTER NINE

As busy as I was during that time, my thoughts were always consumed by one tall gentleman with dark, penetrating eyes. I wondered when I might see him again. Mama, of course, noticed my daydreaming. As we stood there paring potatoes for the evening's supper, she asked, "Are you okay, Anna? You seem a bit distracted lately."

"Mama, how did you know you were in love with Papa?"

Mama turned to me, wiping her hands on her apron. "Ah...so that's it. I know you and Ella both got eyes for our newcomer, Mr. Fletcher." Mama was a very smart woman and knew that Mr. Fletcher had his eye on me, not Ella. Not that my sister wasn't pleasant to look at. Like I said, Ella resembled Papa with her dark hair and blue eyes, while I resembled Mama, who was fair with blonde hair and green eyes. Ella was tall while I was on the short side. Mama said, "Anna, I understand that Joe seems different than the men we're used to here, and that makes him seem exciting, but I don't know that what *you're* feeling is actual love. You're very young and you just met the man!"

"But how *did* you know Papa was the one you wanted to marry?"

"I don't know," she said and smiled, turning back to her potatoes, "I just did."

CHAPTER TEN

Joe finally came back on a Saturday morning, looking more like he belonged in West Langford, with his denim overalls and soft gray cap upon his head. He was beaming, and I got happy just looking at him. He approached me first, as I was already outside with Lonny and Doug, coming back from the chicken coop after gathering eggs for tomorrow's breakfast. "Anna!" he exclaimed and moved quickly toward me, caressing my shoulders. His dark eyes looked so intense… "It's official! I'm now the owner of my own farm. Where's your father? I need to talk to him right away." I looked at my brothers, who were just standing there like they were invisible.

"Where *is* Papa?" I asked.

Doug answered, "I think he's in the barn checking Molly to see if that medicine Doc Hayes brought over is working."

Lonny nodded and confirmed, "Yup; that's where he is, all right."

"Come on, Joe; I'll take you on over," I said as I handed my basket of eggs to Doug.

Papa looked up when he heard us enter the barn. I could see he was tending to Molly. While Joe's farmer clothes looked new and unworn, Papa's clothes looked ragged in comparison. His shirt was dirty, his pants had a hole in the knee—*I'll have to tell Mama about that so she can patch it up,* I thought—and his work boots were muddy and grimy. "Hey, Joe! Good to see you! How'd things go in Bradford?"

"Great, Elmer. I was just telling Anna I own Mary's farm now. It's all mine."

"Well, good for you, Joe. Like I said, I'll help you any way I can. I'll even spare my boys to help you out a couple days a week if need be. When do you want to go meet Buddy? He's been waiting on you to get back."

"I'm ready anytime…I'm eager to get started. Most of my things have already arrived from Louisiana. Just need to get everything in order."

"Okay, let me just finish up here with Molly and we can go on over to his place." He bent back down and put more salve on Molly's udder.

Buster was by my father's side but came over and licked my hand. "Good Busty," I said, giving him a pat.

"Thanks, Elmer," Joe replied, "I appreciate it. By the way, how *is* Molly?"

Looking back up at Joe, he said, "Doc Hayes is a good animal doctor, Joe. Anytime your animals need doctorin', he's the one to call on. She's healing up just fine."

I was very pleased that the medicine Dr. Hayes brought over seemed to be helping Molly and she didn't seem to be in as much pain. Doc had told Papa to give her another week and she'd be good as new.

"Good ta know, Elmer; I'll be sure and take your advice."

Joe looked at me and pulled me outside. Staring down into my eyes, he said quietly, "I'd forgotten just how pretty you are, Anna. I couldn't wait to get back here. I brought y'all a present from Bradford. I'll ask Elmer if I can come calling tonight to bring it to ya."

"Of course," I blushed and said. "But really, Joe? You got me a present? No one's ever bought me a present 'cept Mama and Papa." My heart was ready to explode…it fluttered.

"Yes, *really*," he said, amused, his dimples making him look like a young boy. "I hope ya like it."

I smiled and thought, *Yes, Mama, I DO think this is love!* He was just so darn cute!

Papa invited Joe for supper when he found out Joe wanted to come calling, so Joe got there very early. I heard the dogs barking outside but thought they saw a squirrel or some other kind of critter. It startled me when I heard Joe call out, "Hello there, y'all; can I come in?"

Mama glanced at me and said, "Sure, Joe; come on in."

After paying his respects and being the Southern gentleman that he was, he asked Mama for permission to take me for a walk around the yard for a spell before it was time to eat. Since I was in the middle of cutting up vegetables for the stew Mama was preparing, I looked at her with a question in my eyes. She looked at a frowning Ella first, sighed, and said, "That's fine. Ella and I will finish up here." If looks could kill, I would be a goner by the way Ella glared at me.

It was still pretty light out, but dusk was almost upon us. I was nervous as Joe guided me to the cow barn. He sat me down on a milking stool and handed me a large package. Molly proceeded to make her presence known, and one of our other cows answered. Because I was nervous, I said, "Hush now." Not that their voices weren't calming to me, but I felt the need to say something. The package was rectangular in shape and quite heavy. I looked at him before opening it and nervously gave him my best smile. The brown wrapping was easy to tear apart, and I opened it slowly and carefully. I looked up at him in surprise. His smile back at me looked like sunshine. The gift was a big, black Bible with embossed gold lettering. *Well, I have to admit…I wasn't expecting this!* I thought.

He said, "Anna, from the first time I laid eyes on you, I knew I wanted you. Now I know we have to keep this a secret for a while 'cause I know your Mama will say it's much too soon, but I just wanted you to know that you are in my future plans. Your Papa tole me I needed a good wife to help and support me as a farmer, and I just know you're the one for me. This here Bible will be our family Bible to record all our children and their children and their children's children. You don't have to say anything now, 'cause like I said, we just met and all, but I want you to think about me and being my wife and having my children."

Well, gosh almighty! What do I say? Think about him?? I think about him all the time! But I said, "Okay, Joe…I'll think about that. Thank you for the Bible. I'll treasure it always. But now, let's go eat some of Mama's delicious stew." And we did. But all through supper, while the menfolk talked about farming, my thoughts were on what it *would* be like being Mrs. Joe Fletcher.

CHAPTER ELEVEN

Buddy had delivered Mary and her children safely to Doris and told us they had settled into a nice little place that even had a small yard where the kids could play. Joe was now our new neighbor, although I hardly ever saw him. Since Papa or one of my brothers seemed to be spending more time with Joe than I was, suppertime was the highlight of my day, listening to them tell of Joe and how he was learning the ins and outs of farming. Mary's farm needed a lot of work, and Buddy and Joe were doing repairs as well as trying to keep the farm working. Papa said he invited Joe to supper a couple of times, but Joe declined because by the end of most days, he was too tired to do anything but go to bed. I missed his eyes and his generous smile. I asked Papa if Joe seemed happy with farming, and he said, "Yes, I do believe he is. It's kind of like that boy is on a mission to accomplish something, and Buddy and I agree that he's smart and a quick learner." That made me proud.

Weeks went by, and I turned fifteen. It was hard to believe that soon, Leo and I would once again be walking to school together every day. The day after my birthday, I asked if it would be all right if I took some of the previous night's meal over to Joe since I was sure he mustn't be eating properly. Mama had made one of her famous pot roasts. She knew it was a favorite of mine, and I told her I really wanted to share it with him. The real reason was that I missed him and thought it was a good excuse to go visit him. "Why, of course, Anna; that's very thoughtful of you. I think it's a good idea." While Mama got out a basket and started loading it, I got my bonnet and shawl, and with Mama's permission, I went to the root cellar to fetch some canned vegetables and fruit to add to the basket. Bringing my cart up close to the kitchen door, I loaded the food with Mama's help. It was a beautiful September day. The leaves were starting to turn into the magical array of vibrant colors that graced our town every fall. I loved everything about the fall; the smells and the clear, cool air made me feel alive. It was my favorite season. I inhaled deeply and smiled. As I walked along the rocky road, though, I wondered whether Joe would be happy to see me. The butterflies were back in my stomach as I anticipated his reaction. What if he changed his mind about me and that was the real reason he wasn't accepting Papa's invitations? Deep in thought and not paying much attention to what was ahead of me, I heard someone laugh. Looking up, I saw Leo walking toward me. Leo had filled out. No longer the skinny, childish crazy kid, he was tall, nice-looking, and levelheaded. His voice was also much deeper than it used to be. "Hey, Anna, where you headed?" He laughed again. "You look like you got the weight of the world on your shoulders."

"Oh, hey, Leo, I didn't see you coming." I was always happy to see Leo. "Goin' to Joe's place to bring him and Buddy some food," I replied. "Where *you* headed?"

Looking surprised and concerned about my answer, no longer laughing, he said, "Actually, I was headed to see if I could borrow a sickle from your Pa. My uncle is here to help us with harvesting the corn, and we need an extra one."

"Oh, well, I'm sure that would be okay. You'll find Papa with the boys in the upper field picking apples, but you know Papa has lots of tools and I'm sure he'd be able to spare one."

Leo just looked at me kind of sadly and said, "Hope you had a happy birthday yesterday, Anna. Seems like we don't get to spend much time together anymore." The truth was, I was purposely avoiding Leo with the thought in my head that I had outgrown him.

Feeling a tad guilty, I said, "Thanks for remembering my birthday, Leo. Umm…well, school starts next week, so I'll be seeing you *there* every day. We can walk together like we always have."

That seemed to cheer him up a bit. "Okay, Anna. That sounds good to me. Well, I better get going. They're waitin' on me for that sickle." Leo's father had a small farm like Joe's. Since Leo only had sisters, other family members often came to help at certain times of the year. He turned and started walking again toward my house, but after a few seconds, he turned around and said, "Anna?"

I also turned. "Yeah?"

He looked on over to Joe's place, hesitated, shook his head, and said, "Never mind."

CHAPTER TWELVE

When I got to the farm, the first person I saw was Buddy. He was busy repairing a stone wall that had been falling down ever since I could remember. He looked very intent as he worked, hauling huge rocks and placing them just right. It took him a moment to see I was coming toward him. Looking up, he said, "Oh, hey, Anna! How you doin' today?" Even though the air was cool, I could see the sweat stains on his dirty light blue shirt. He looked mighty tired too.

"Hey, Buddy! I'm doing good...how 'bout you?"

"Oh, I'm good. Just realizing I ain't as young as I used to be...or as strong, for that matter!" He chuckled. "What's that you got in your cart? Do I see one of your Mama's prize-winnin' pies?"

"Why, you sure do, Buddy. Thought you and Joe would appreciate some of Mama's good homemade cooking."

"You are an angel of mercy, girl! You'd better go on in the house with that stuff before I quit working and devour that pie before Joe even gets a chance to see it."

I laughed. "Okay, Buddy. Where is Joe, anyway?"

"He should be in the chicken coop getting those hens ready for the winter months. Told him he needed to get more straw down and take care of their nesting boxes."

"He sure is lucky to have you, Buddy."

He put his hands out to his sides, arched his back, and stretched. "Well, thank you, Anna. I'm glad to help out. You be sure and thank your Mama for all the goodies. Joe and I are gonna eat good today!"

"You bet I will, Buddy. I'll see ya later."

Joe told me years later that one day when he and Buddy were working side by side, he asked him why he quit farming his own land. Buddy explained that because his farm was so small, he wasn't making enough money to make a living. He felt as though he was working too hard for nothing. But because he enjoyed farming, he figured he'd hire himself out to help other farmers in the area. He admitted to Joe that it had been a good decision for him and Cora since they never really had much money. When Joe told me that story, I told him that I was glad we were able to help Cora and Buddy because they were such good folks. Joe always agreed that Buddy was a godsend to us.

After placing the food on the kitchen counter, I went in search of Joe. As I approached the coop, I could hear a lot of muttering and a few cuss words. I heard a chicken squawk like it was in pain and I thought, *Did Joe just kick one of the chickens?* I figured it would be a good idea to warn him I was coming, so I yelled, "Hey, Joe; it's me, Anna!"

"Anna? Come on in." He was facing the door as I entered. My heart went out to him as I took him in from head to toe. His hair was mussed and dirty and he looked as if he hadn't shaved in a few days. His eyes looked tired, but he managed to smile and looked genuinely happy to see me.

"Hey, Joe. How've you been?" I asked, relieved to see him smiling as the chickens ran all around, clucking and making a racket.

"Well, now that I see you, I'm feeling much better. Never knew chickens were such dirty, smelly things, I'll tell ya that! Come closer. I've missed ya, Anna. Your Pa was right…farming ain't no easy business. I don't think I've ever worked this hard in all my life. There's so much involved every day. So much to learn! I'm sure thankful that your Pa hooked me up with Buddy. He's been a dang good teacher." He smiled. "I'm sure there are days he'd like to tell me to just go on back to Louisiana and leave farming to Vermonters who actually know what they're doing!" I laughed. His smile suddenly gone, he said, "I am sorry I ain't been around to see you, Anna, but at the end of my chores around here, I just want to find my bed. I'm doing all this for *us*; you know that, right? You been okay?"

I took a couple of steps closer and stopped when I got a whiff. "Whoa, Joe, seems like you smell just about as bad as these here chickens." I giggled. He didn't smile back, so I spoke quickly, afraid that I offended him. "I've been just fine. I brought you and Buddy some of Mama's food you like so well so you can have a decent meal tonight. Hopefully, you won't be too tired to eat it." I smiled tentatively.

His frown left, and he said with his Southern drawl, "I don't think anything could keep me from eating your Mama's cooking. That was mighty thoughtful of her. You be sure to thank her for me. I'm ready to quit working right now and go get a taste!"

I wasn't about to tell him it was my idea, so I said, "I sure will, Joe…I'll tell her, but don't be too long to eat it. I left everything on your kitchen counter and don't want anything to spoil."

"Almost finished with this here chicken coop. Then I'll fetch Buddy and we'll eat our fill." He hesitated only a moment before saying, "Actually, Anna, I've been thinking about you a lot and was hoping to come calling on you Friday evening. I promise I'll take a bath and smell better when I come." He grinned slowly, showing his dimples. "Would that be all right?"

"I'd like that very much, Joe," I replied with my own grin. "Come for supper…I'll tell Mama and Papa!"

"Well, all right, then. Thanks for stopping by and bringing us some decent food. I'm 'bout sick and tired of canned beans! And ya know? Suddenly, these chickens don't seem like such bad creatures after all. You sure know how to make things better for me, Anna."

I chuckled, "Bye, Joe…see ya Friday."

As I headed home, I sighed deeply, relieved that nothing had changed. I wondered if I was going to meet Leo on my way home, but he was nowhere in sight. He was probably already back at his farm. I got to thinking about the way he looked when I told him I was on my way to Joe's. I couldn't figure out why he disliked Joe so much. Seemed like everyone else took a liking to him. I let the question go and my thoughts returned to Joe, anticipating Friday evening, and wondering why he looked at me strangely when I teased him about being smelly. Leo would have laughed out loud. I thought, *Men sure can be confusing.*

CHAPTER THIRTEEN

Friday came quickly enough, and I made sure I helped Mama prepare the meal. We were having fried chicken, mashed potatoes, our garden turnips, Mama's homemade bread, and of course, as with every one of our meals, homemade pickles. I churned some fresh butter that afternoon and made Mama's special chocolate cake for dessert with cream sugar frosting. Whenever Mama made her cake, there was always a dip in the middle. When Ella made it, there was no dip, but I was happy when mine came out of the oven and it looked exactly like Mama's. Whoever got those middle pieces were rewarded with extra frosting, because we always filled up the dip so the cake would look even. I was going to make sure Joe got one of those pieces.

For my birthday, Mama had made me a new dress. It was emerald green to match my eyes, and I couldn't wait to wear it tonight. Instead of wearing my hair up, as I usually did most days to keep it out of the way while I did my chores, I wore my long, blonde ringlets down. When I came downstairs that evening, Papa actually whistled at me. Lonny said, "Well, look at Anna. She's all growed up." Doug chuckled, and Ella just wore her sourpuss face.

Mama smiled and said, "You look lovely, Anna."

"Thanks, Mama."

When the dogs started barking, I knew Joe had arrived. More butterflies. Would *he* think I looked pretty? I wondered.

Papa went out to greet him and they were out there a spell, I assumed talking farming. I was setting the table when they walked through the door. Joe looked quite handsome in his Louisiana clothes. He had shaved and his hair was neatly combed.

"Wow, Anna, you are a vision," he exclaimed as he walked through the door. He stared at me, wide-eyed. At that moment, he must have realized he hadn't addressed Mama yet. Recovering quickly, he said, "Sorry, Mrs. Roberts…how y'all doing this evening? I have to thank you for sending over that delicious food the other day. I had to fight Buddy for the last piece of pie."

"You're very welcome, Joe. Actually, it was Anna's idea to feed you. I think she was worried about you."

Joe looked over at me with surprise in his eyes. "Well, it was much appreciated. Like I said before, a man could certainly get spoiled eating like *that* every day. By the way, as usual, it smells delicious in here. I brought my appetite with me," he said, looking at me and making me blush.

I thought, *Leo was right. He does look like he wants to eat me up.* I found out that evening that fried chicken was his favorite meal. His Ma used to make it for him when he was a little boy. I did wonder if he was comparing Mama's chicken to his mother's recipe, but if he was, he didn't show it because he had seconds. Mama said we should wait a while before we had cake, so we'd all have room in our bellies to really enjoy it. The boys excused themselves and said they had to go check on something in the barn, but they would definitely be back for cake.

Ella and I helped Mama clean up the dishes and put the leftover food away while Joe and Papa talked their men talk. By the time we finished our cleaning, Lonny and Doug were back, and I served the cake and coffee.

Once again, as we were enjoying our dessert, the conversation consisted mostly of farming. Now that he knew how much was involved in running a farm, Joe decided not to raise sheep right away. He had his hands full repairing Mary's farm and taking care of the chickens and cows—not to mention the gardening and haying and everything else. Apple season was upon us, and that was one more thing to learn. He was actually happy he only had one small orchard to take care of. Buddy knew so many people in our town, and he talked Joe into hiring some young boys to do the picking. Joe said he was eternally grateful for Buddy and thanked Papa again and again for bringing Buddy into his life. Joe also wanted to learn the process of sugaring. Papa told him that it took about forty gallons of sap to make only one gallon of maple syrup. Sugaring was done in the early spring, after the winter thaw, and was a lot of work in the beginning because you had to tap the maple trees, hang the buckets, and clear the path from tree to tree so there was room for the sled with the gathering tub.

Joe told Papa he definitely wanted to make syrup because it was the sweetest and most delicious syrup he'd ever eaten, and he was eager to try his hand at it. Buddy was going to walk him through it come spring. Maybe when he got a better handle on things, he said, he'd get some sheep. Papa agreed and said, "I think that's a smart decision, Joe."

Joe also told us about his decision to hire someone to do the cooking, cleaning, and laundry. He and Buddy had no time for things like that.

Buddy's sister, Cora, said she'd come three days a week to help out. He told us he was supposed to meet up with her on Monday, and if all went well, she would start helping immediately. Cora was a mothering type, and I felt better knowing she would take care of Joe. "I hope Cora can make a cake as fine as this, Mrs. Roberts!" Joe exclaimed.

"Oh, I didn't make the cake, Joe. Anna did," Mama admitted.

I was quick to answer as Joe looked at me. "But it's Mama's recipe."

With admiration in his eyes, he said, "Well, it's one of the best-tasting cakes *I* ever ate!"

Humbly, I said, "Thanks, Joe."

As I got up to help with the dessert dishes, Mama suggested that the two of us go sit on the front porch. She knew Joe wasn't there for her cooking alone. I usually helped Mama clean up, but I was happy to go be alone with Joe. She also dismissed Ella. I know she did that to be kind and fair. She knew it was hard on Ella that Joe was interested in me and not her. That was Mama. Papa and the boys went to go check on the lamp for the hens. Now that the days were shorter, they had to trick the hens with fake daylight so they would lay their eggs normally.

Sugarhouse Trials

Joe and I walked through the parlor to the front door. The night was dark, but the stars shone brightly. I inhaled the pungent smell of the leaves, which were just beginning to drop off the trees. I felt alive and excited.

We sat in the two rockers that had been on the porch since I was born, looking out over the yard. I could hear the peepers as they sang their nightly lullaby, and the fireflies looked like little diamonds lighting up the bushes.

Joe broke the silence and told me how pretty I looked. "Your hair is beautiful, Anna. You should wear it down more often. I like it." At that, I told myself I would wear it down whenever I was with him. "Now, tell me what's been going on in your life lately."

"Well, I turned fifteen the day before I brought you the food."

"Ya did? Why didn't y'all say something?"

"I don't know…it didn't seem important."

"Everything about you is important to me, Anna. Please know that. If I had known, I would've got you a birthday present." The way he looked at me, made me melt in my chair. "What else?" he asked sincerely.

"I start back to school next week. It'll be my last year at Miss Everdeen's."

"That's good! We have a year to get to really know each other before I ask your Pa if I can marry you." I was glad it was dark so he couldn't see my face. I felt like I was going to explode. Joe said, "If I had my druthers, I'd marry you tomorrow, but I know your Mama would never go for that." He chuckled. "I'd much rather have *you* in my kitchen than Cora, especially now that I've tasted that cake!" he teased. "But tonight, we're gonna talk and get to know each other better. I imagine you must have lots of questions about me and my past life, so I need ta tell you a little bit about myself. We haven't had much time to talk about things like that, and it's important. I think your Pa and brothers know more about me than you do."

"I'd like that a lot, Joe," I said with a shy smile.

"Okay. Here goes. I was brought up in a city called Shreveport. It's much bigger than your little town, West Langford. Like your own Pa, my father inherited the house that's been in our family forever. My daddy was in the cotton business and did well for himself. Because he had a little money, he was able to buy a cotton gin. It made him a rich man, Anna. He and my mother had five children, all boys, me being the youngest. My older brothers were interested in following in my father's footsteps, but cotton never appealed to me. There were slaves involved, and I always thought that all men should be free. Some of my father's slaves became good friends of mine. They were good, hard-working men, and I thought it unfair that just because their skin was darker than ours, that they should have to serve us."

I had never seen a dark person before, but at school, we learned a bit about slavery and did see pictures. I guess because there was nothing like that here in West Langford, I didn't give it much thought, but I did like what Joe was saying. I kept listening…

"Because I was privileged, I was able to go to high school, and that's where I met my wife, Melanie. Her daddy was also in the cotton business, so we had much in common. I could have gone on to college if I wanted to, but she and I got married right after we graduated and she got pregnant pretty quick. My Pa had set us up in the guesthouse, and even though my heart wasn't into it, I worked for him loading and unloading the cotton from the steamboats that came down the river from Texas. We were happy enough, but Mel didn't have an easy pregnancy. She was sick most of the time, and by the end of her pregnancy, she went to live with her Mama, who wanted to take care of her. When the baby decided to come, it was a long process. I was there with her Daddy in the next room, listening to her screams and cries. It was horrible. The midwife was having a difficult time trying to get the baby to come out, and Melanie ended up bleeding to death. It was the worst night of my life. I could tell by the way her parents looked at me that they blamed me. Hell, *I* blamed me. They finally got the little fellow out of her, but the damage had been done. He lasted two days but wasn't able to breathe properly. We named him Daniel after Mel's father and buried him next to his Mama."

Joe was quiet for a moment, and I reached over to take his hand. "I'm so sorry, Joe. That must have been awful for you." I noticed Joe had started rocking in his chair harder and faster as he told his story.

"Yeah, it was pretty bad. I stuck it out working for my father for a couple of years, but I was very angry and unhappy. One of the men I met unloading the boats told me about Vermont. He grew up here and said the people were really friendly and farming was the way to go. Made a man feel like a man. It piqued my interest, and I read up on it. Decided that's what I wanted to do. So, I saved my money and told my parents about my plans. They were skeptical at first. I think they thought it was just a whim because I was grieving, but they thought maybe doing something other than cotton and being away from Louisiana might be good for me and change my attitude. I guess I wasn't much fun to be around. Every day as I read more about Vermont, I kept getting more excited about my new adventure. So, at the age of twenty-three, here I am starting a new life, finally making my dream come true. When my parents realized just how serious I was, my father told me he would help me buy a farm...said it was an investment. You'll get to meet them one day since they told me they planned on checking up on their investment once I was settled and all." He smiled, stopped rocking, and looked at me. "You'll like them, Anna, and they'll love you! Anyway, when I saw you at Sam's store, you were like the icing on my cake. I just knew I was meant to be here. With you, Anna."

Not long after, Joe got up and told me he'd better head back to the farm because the stupid rooster he had always woke him up at the crack of dawn. He admitted that it was probably a good thing since there was so much to do first thing in the morning. "Buddy's already there working by the time I walk out of the house every morning."

As we said our good-byes, I got another kiss on the cheek, so I kissed him back on his cheek. He smiled his boyish smile and said, "You sure are something special, Miss Anna Roberts."

When I got into bed that night, I thought and thought about what a different life Joe led before coming here to West Langford. It seemed as though he had already lived a whole 'nother lifetime! I was glad he told me his story, and I felt I knew him better now. I couldn't wait to share his story with Mama tomorrow.

CHAPTER FOURTEEN

School was school. I have always enjoyed learning, and from what Miss Everdeen said, I was easy to teach. But this year seemed different. It was hard to concentrate, and more than once, I wondered if I really needed schooling since I was to be a farmer's wife. Mama didn't go to school as many years as I had, and she did just fine. But every day, Leo and I would make the trek up the hill and sit with all the other kids learning our lessons. Leo didn't talk as much anymore, which was okay with me. Mostly, we walked in silence thinking to ourselves. I still considered him my best friend, but things were different now. We weren't little kids anymore. And I was glad he finally stopped asking me so many questions about Joe.

Now that Joe and I were officially a couple, we spent more time together. Mama allowed me to go to his farm to help Cora whenever my schoolwork and chores were done. I looked forward to those days because not only could I pretend to live there, but I always made it a point to find Joe, wherever he was, to bring him a drink or something I made for him. He'd always take a little break and sit with me a spell, and we'd talk about things going on in our lives. I have to admit I did speed up my chores and skimmed my homework so I could spend more time with him. Often, we would tend to the chickens together, or pick vegetables or apples together, whatever needed to be done where I could help. I already considered it "our" farm and loved working it and getting to know my future husband. One day, he caught me off guard.

"How many children do you want, Anna?"

"Umm..." I gulped. "I guess I never really gave it much thought."

"Well, I want at least a dozen!" he said seriously.

"Oh!"

"I'm teasing you, Anna. I think four or five will do. I'll want a son, but it would be pleasing to me to see a bunch of little Annas running around the house as decorations."

"Ha...you are funny, Joe!"

I quickly learned that Joe was a very proud, independent man. That was the main reason he wasn't keen on working his father's cotton business. He wanted to make his own way, be his own person, and make a life that he could take credit for. I admired him and felt privileged that he would choose me, Anna, as his wife and co-worker. Papa always told me that I had my own mind, like Lonny. Unlike Ella, I sometimes could be very defiant when I was told to do things I didn't agree with. I also wanted to be my own person. Yes, I thought, we *were* meant to be together. We made a perfect couple.

The next month, October, Ella started to be courted by one of the farmers who lived in East Kent. His name was Lewis Shaver and because everyone was familiar with each other in all the surrounding towns, we knew him to be a good man. Lewis was about twenty-nine, and like some of the farmers around here—my own brothers included—he was always too busy to go looking for a wife. He was a jolly man with kind eyes, curly brown hair, and a beard to match. We all liked him very much. His father had recently handed over the farm to him, and Lewis came to ask Papa if he could borrow Ol' Charlie for breeding purposes. Ella just happened to be in the garden that day. He musta liked the look of her, because after that first visit, he seemed to come more frequently. When he came around, Ella smiled and laughed and seemed to be a much happier person. She was seventeen and I know she was afraid she was going to end up an old maid like Miss Everdeen. I think it especially bothered her that I had a beau and she didn't. So, when Lewis started paying attention to her, she changed and became a nicer person, and I even began to like her a little. They courted only a few months and then announced their engagement. It was going to be a May wedding, and she and Mama were busy making all the arrangements. That left extra chores for me to do, which was fine since I was thinking that these were better lessons for me to learn in order to be a good wife to Joe.

Joe was getting better at farming, but I could tell it still wore him out. Even though he was tired, he made it a point of trying to come for supper once a week. After all, Lewis had *his* own farm and managed to eat supper with us every week. Joe and Lewis were sort of becoming friends, but I got the impression Joe viewed him somehow like competition. Like Buddy and Papa, Lewis was always willing to help Joe with problem-solving, but I noticed that as with Leo, Joe wasn't always receptive to the advice Lewis gave him.

One beautiful early spring day, the four of us went on a picnic together. It was shortly before Ella's wedding day. After a harsh winter, the green was refreshing. Buds were sprouting, birds were chirping, and the early flowers were poking their way through the earth. We took a hay wagon and meandered down River Road. It followed the Woods River, and it was a beautiful ride. Scattered rock maple trees lined the road as well as the many mossy stone walls built so many years ago. We found a nice grassy spot and laid our blanket down under a huge tree that Lewis said was probably over 100 years old. I was a little shocked when Joe questioned Lewis, "How do *you* know this tree is over a hundred years old? Are you a tree expert?"

I thought, *Why is Joe questioning Lewis with that tone of voice?* Ella and I looked at each other. I could tell she was also wondering about Joe's accusing question.

Luckily, Lewis didn't notice. "No, not by any means, Joe," Lewis answered amicably. "I'm just assuming it is because of the size and all. I'm far from a tree expert." Ella and I laughed it off so as not to make a big deal about it.

After that, Joe loosened up, and we had fun while we played Blind Man's Bluff and ate the Johnny cakes, fresh creamy cheeses, and the desserts Ella and I had packed. We sipped lemonade and talked about nothing important. The four of us were young and in love. Life was good, and I was getting closer to graduating from Miss Everdeen's school.

CHAPTER FIFTEEN

It was a lovely day at the end of May when my sister got married. The forsythia and crocuses were everywhere, the trees had buds, the lilac bushes were in full bloom, and baby animals were being born right and left. I thought spring seemed like a good time for a wedding...new beginnings and all. Joe was planning on asking Papa for my hand that very day after the festivities...told me Papa would be in a good mood after drinking hard cider all day.

Ella had a good-sized wedding. All the neighbors were invited, and many of the women, as was the custom in West Langford, pitched in with their favorite dishes. Papa and the boys set up tables, and Lonny's friend, Orrin, and his wife, Barb, brought their guitars and were able to get the crowd singing all the favorite songs of the time. The afternoon was animated and so much fun. Joe didn't arrive in time for the vows, and I was worried he might not be able to attend the wedding at all because of something that may have happened at the farm. Cora sat next to me on one side and

Leo sat on my other side. Not wanting Leo to hear, I quietly asked Cora if she knew why Joe wasn't there. She replied, "I have no idea, Anna. I know Buddy is here. I saw him over talking to John Hood a while ago."

I frowned, wondering if Joe was okay and whether I should send Lonny or Doug to go looking for him. But while we were all laughing, joking, and enjoying all the tasty dishes, I sensed his presence next to me. I looked up at him and smiled. "Hey, Joe...everything okay?" At the sight of Joe, Leo quietly got up and left. Joe immediately took his place.

The way Joe was looking at me brought out the blush in my cheeks. "Sorry, Anna. I had to meet a man in Benson about an animal I'm interested in buying. Didn't think it would take as long as it did. Did I miss much?"

Now that Joe and I were spending so much time together, I felt more comfortable around him and enjoyed teasing him. "Well, Mr. Joe Fletcher, you didn't miss the food, and knowing you, that would be the worst thing to miss!" I laughed.

"Ha! You know me well, Miss Anna Roberts!" Under his breath, he added, "Soon to be Mrs. Anna Fletcher."

I looked at him looking at me with that "eat you up" look and said, "Well, come on! Dig in and eat some of this good Vermont food. Mrs. Hood makes the best potato salad you've ever eaten, and Mrs. Smith outdid herself with her corn casserole."

Joe filled his plate and started eating like there was no tomorrow. I just watched and smiled.

After filling his stomach, he turned to me, focusing hungrily on my lips and said, "By the way, Anna, you look ravishing." Since

Sugarhouse Trials

I was Ella's witness—or what people were now starting to call a bridesmaid—I was wearing a modest light-green dress with a dropped waist that was all the fashion.

Because I was a little embarrassed, I answered in my best Southern drawl, "Whah thank ya, kind suh…y'all are a true gentleman."

Joe laughed and said, "Whah ma'am, y'all got that accent down jes fine and dandy." We laughed and I was so glad he was here with me. He was a good dancer and sang a few songs with Orrin. Everyone liked Joe, and I was so proud of him. I couldn't wait for it to be our turn to be the bride and groom.

Later that evening, when people were starting to clean up and the younger families were leaving to tuck their children into bed, Joe whispered in my ear, "Time to be a man and ask for my wife…wish me luck, darlin'."

Of course, Papa said yes. Cider or no cider, Papa liked Joe and thought we'd make a good match. Lonny had also been enjoying cider that day. When Lonny heard the news, he came to me. "I'm really happy for ya, Anna girl," he slurred, "but it's funny, I really thought that you and Leo would get married someday. Don't look at me like that…I really like Joe, but I don't know, you and Leo…" He gave me a strong hug, winked at me, and said, "Be happy, lil sis."

I was shocked. *Me and Leo? Married? No.* To me, it would be like marrying my brother Doug. Leo and I never had that kind of relationship. I put that thought out of my mind. How odd Lonny would even think of that. My heart belonged to Joe.

CHAPTER SIXTEEN

Time went on, and it didn't seem too long afterward that I became an aunt. It made me feel older. Ella's first child was a girl, and she named her Emma after Mama. Both Mama and Papa were excited to be grandparents for the first time, so they both spent a lot of time in East Kent that February. At the time, Lonny and Doug, both being single, were able to handle the farm while Papa got used to his new role as Grampa.

Emma was not a very happy baby. Every time I went to visit, someone was trying to rock her or walk her to try and stop her from crying. Mama said she had colic. I didn't know what that meant, but I did know that if I had kids, I sure didn't want them to have colic!

Joe and I had decided to wait until October of the next year to get married. When Joe found out it was my favorite time of year, he insisted we would celebrate our day when West Langford was at its best. Joe thought it would be better to wait the year before taking our vows so that he could be in a better position with the farm. He still had much to learn and didn't want to take away from our time together because he was still learning "the art of farming." Mama liked the idea because she said it would give us more time to get to know each other. She also commented that in her opinion, it would give us both time to become wiser and more mature.

Buddy also agreed that the fall would be a good time for the wedding because the haying would be finished, and it would pretty much only be our potatoes and corn that would need harvesting. Apple picking would commence shortly after harvesting, but by then we should be settled and back to a routine. I couldn't wait to play house and be a help to Joe every day. It seemed so far away.

Now that Ella was off in her own home, my daily life that year became much busier. Now I was solely responsible for the chickens and the milking when Papa needed help. I felt bad for Lonny and Doug because once I left, no longer would I be able to take on some of their responsibilities. I was afraid it would be left to Mama. I also knew that Mama would miss me fiercely with the household duties. Part of me felt guilty because she wouldn't have anyone to help her. "Mama, how are you ever gonna do everything yourself?"

"Don't you be worrying about me, Anna. Papa and I talked about it and thought we'd ask Cora to come by, at least on Mondays, to do the laundry. You and Joe won't need her every day once you settle in. I'm sure you'll still want her help, but I'm pretty sure she'd be willing to help both of us."

Sugarhouse Trials

"That's a great idea, Mama. I'm sure she'd be happy to do that." And she was. Cora told Mama and me that when she helped us, she felt needed, and if a person felt needed, that person was a happy person.

Mama also insisted that I start making most of the meals. She wanted me to feel comfortable in the kitchen and figured I needed the practice. Pretty soon Papa couldn't tell the difference between my pot roast and Mama's. Joe still tried to come for supper once a week, although there were times when it wasn't possible. We both missed spending as much time together but consoled ourselves, knowing that soon we'd be spending the rest of our lives together.

So, time went on, day after day, week after week, month after month. Joe and I both got better at the things necessary to make our life and farm run smoothly. Both Buddy and Cora were always a huge help, and Joe paid them well. We decided that once we were married, with the exception of Mondays, Cora could come and help me whenever I needed her or whenever she wanted to. I helped her fix up the bedroom next to ours with the thought it might be a nursery someday. She was thrilled that one day she might take on another job…being a nanny. In the meantime, once Joe and I were married, it would be her bedroom. She would still have to make sure Buddy was taken care of, but I think she was looking forward to having another woman to talk to on a regular basis. I noticed a big change in Cora. When I first met her, she used to stiffen up when I hugged her. Now, she was the one who initiated hugs, and her hugs were always sincere. We were becoming very close.

Lenore Sylvain Dexter

One day, I asked Cora about her and Buddy. She confided in me and told me that there were five years between them. "When I was five and Buddy was ten, our mother got cholera. Papa took care of her, and it wasn't long after that when he came down with it. They refused to let Buddy and me get anywhere near them for fear we would get the disease. Even though Buddy went and fetched the doctor, it was too late and both our parents died within days of each other. From then on, Buddy took care of me like he was my own Papa. Only ten years old and he was able to care for me and the farm. I remember one day, some important-looking people came and wanted to take us away, but Buddy called on your Grandfather Ev for help. Ev talked to the people and assured them that he and his wife, Katherine, would be willing to take responsibility for the two of us. Your grandparents let us stay on our own farm because that's what Buddy wanted, but they were always close in case we needed them. Your Gramma Katherine showed me how to do lots of things that my Mama would have taught me if she had lived. Likewise, your Grandpa Ev was a huge help to Buddy. Because our farm was small, Buddy was able to handle it with the help of your Grampa and your dad and his brothers. Your Gramma would bring over food once in a while, and once a year she would sew me a new dress on my birthday. She was the one who taught *me* to sew. Then I was able to sew my own clothes and Buddy's, too. Yes, we owe a lot to you Roberts people."

"Wow," I said thoughtfully. "I wonder how come no one ever told me that story. I see my grandparents' picture every day in my Pa's office, and they always looked mean and unfriendly to me."

Sugarhouse Trials

"Not hardly, Anna. They weren't much for hugging and sentiments and all, but neither were Buddy and I, so that made no difference. Your Gramma once told me, 'Actions speak louder than words.' I never forgot that."

"Wow," I said again. I was happy Cora told me her story, and I still wondered why I hadn't heard about my grandparents from my own family. From now on, I would look at their picture in Papa's office in a whole new way.

CHAPTER SEVENTEEN

Our wedding day was rapidly approaching. Joe was excited because his parents would be coming to the wedding. He was proud of what he had accomplished and learned and wanted to share his new life with them. They came about a week before the wedding, taking the train to Rutland. From there, they took the stagecoach through to Sam's store where Buddy picked them up and brought them to Joe's farm. I felt very nervous when Joe introduced me to his parents for the first time. He assured me once again that there was nothing to worry about…they would love me. That still didn't settle my nerves, but I knew it was something I had to do. They were about to become my new family.

I found Joe's mother, Elizabeth, to be a handsome woman. I could see that Joe got his dark eyes from her as she assessed me, the young girl who was about to marry her son. She was quite a bit taller than I was and very dignified; she called Joe "Joseph." At first, I felt intimidated, but when Joe bragged at how I fixed up the farmhouse and made it the homey place she'd noticed and commented on, her face softened and I knew we'd get along just fine. We both loved Joseph Fletcher, and if nothing else, *that* was what we had in common. It had taken me days airing out the musty upstairs bedrooms, washing the linens, placing little trinkets here and there, and making the rooms look cozy and inviting. From the look of things, Mary and Harold hadn't used the upstairs very often. They used the downstairs rooms for their bedrooms. Mama and Cora helped me make new curtains, tablecloths, and quilts, and while it was a lot of work, I was pretty proud when everything was done. This was going to be my home too, and I wanted it to be perfect. Perfect for me and Joe.

Although the house was nowhere as big as The Hermitage, it was plenty big for my taste. The front porch was small but big enough to have two rockers side by side with a small table in between. As you entered the front door, there was a small parlor, where we had a couch and two chairs. There was a wood-burning stove in the corner rather than a fireplace. The parlor led to a big country kitchen, which did have a fireplace. Off the kitchen was the mudroom on one side and a small den-like room on the other side. If you went through the den, there was another room, a bit larger, with a new water closet that Joe and Buddy added off of that. Upstairs, we had three bedrooms that were medium-sized. The one above the kitchen also had a fireplace, so I chose that one for our bedroom. I couldn't wait to share the house with Joe.

Joe's father, Lee, was a kindly man. When we met, he embraced me so hard, I thought my ribs would crack. "Welcome, Daughter; thank you for restoring happiness into Joe's life. I hope the two of you will have many happy years together and bless us with many grandchildren."

Wow! All I could do was smile and think...As long as they don't have colic!

He and Papa had much in common, both being businessmen and all...not to mention their general love for Papa's hard cider. Lee looked like a real city man, all dressed up in his fancy suit. I could see the resemblance between him and Joe, but I still thought Joe favored his mother. Mama and Mrs. Fletcher compared stories of how very different and interesting their lives were. Being a farmer's wife was not at all like being the wife of a cotton tycoon. All in all, Joe and I were pleased that everyone got along, and I began to feel very much at ease with my new family. I was hoping to meet his brothers, but as Joe explained, it was necessary for them to stay behind and run the business. "One of these years, Anna, I'll take you to Shreveport to see where I grew up. You'll see how very different it is from West Langford."

That would be exciting, I thought. *I bet Leo would be jealous!*

CHAPTER EIGHTEEN

Joe spent the week taking his parents here and there, showing them as much of Vermont as they wanted to see. They were very impressed with Joe and his efforts to become a farmer, and I could tell it pleased him. Needless to say, we didn't see much of each other that week, but I had so much to do preparing for our wedding, it was actually a good thing. I also thought it was nice that his parents had him all to themselves since they weren't able to see him very often. I thought if I had a child who moved so far away from me, it would make me very sad and I would relish time alone.

The morning of our wedding threatened rain, and I immediately thought it would be a bad omen if the skies opened up. Mama assured me that the weather did not determine the fate of a marriage. Still, I couldn't help but feel it was unfair that Ella had a beautiful day for *her* wedding. From all the tales I had heard since I was a little girl, I still couldn't help but believe cloudy and rainy *was* a sign of future gloom and doom.

*****

I had to admit Joe and I made a very handsome couple. It was amazing what a couple of years of farming could do to a man's body. No longer did Joe have an adolescent body. He filled out his wedding suit quite nicely, and now it was my turn to look at him like I could "eat *him* up." Mama helped me sew my wedding dress. It was a simple white dress with puffy sleeves that tapered to my wrists. The neckline was high, and my bodice was frilled. I carried a bouquet of multicolored fall flowers. I also wore the same flowers in my hair. Because I knew Joe preferred my hair down, I wore it that way—against Mama's wishes. She said I looked much younger with my hair down.

Of course, I asked Ella to stand up for me, and Joe asked Buddy to stand up for him. As we stood before the minister, Pastor Frank, that late afternoon, I glanced at everyone standing around the room. Everyone looked so serious, I felt like giggling. Joe gazed at me in my parents' parlor as I promised to love and obey him for the rest of our lives. He presented me with a ring, and Pastor Frank declared us married forever in the community and in the eyes of God. Holding my face gently with his hands, Joe whispered in the softest voice, "Close your eyes, Anna." He bent down and kissed me on the lips for the first time and I thought I'd swoon. "You've made me a very happy man," he whispered again, for my ears only. Everyone congratulated us with hugs all around. It was very exciting, but I felt light-headed as I realized I was now Mrs. Joseph Fletcher. I must have worn a goofy grin most of the day.

Even though it was family only, I insisted Leo come. Unfortunately, Leo looked as if he'd rather be anywhere else but there as I was giving my life to Joe, and I wondered if it was a mistake to invite him. He probably also had doubts about attending, because he didn't even stay for the wedding meal. He made an excuse about having to get back to the farm to help his father. When he said his good-byes and thanked us for the invite, his eyes seemed to linger on me a little too long. It made me think for a quick second about what Lonny had said. But I dismissed it right away.

Because it was such a small wedding, we all fit around the family dining table. Papa and the boys had butchered a hog, and Mama prepared all the fixins. She made mashed potatoes; gravy, of course; fresh carrots and peas from the garden; homemade bread with freshly churned butter; homemade cinnamon applesauce; and of course, pickles. The Fletchers were very impressed with the meal, and Joe said, "I told y'all what a great cook Mrs. Roberts is!"

We all joked around and laughed and had a good ol' time, but my thoughts were in the bedroom. Being a farm girl, I knew all about the birds and the bees, but Mama had taken me aside the night before and wanted to know if I had any questions. Being the shy girl that I was, I blushed and said, "No, Mama, I'm pretty sure I know what to expect." I didn't tell her that Ella had taken me aside one day after she married Lewis and told me a lot of details.

"All right, then, my girl; don't be scared. Joe seems gentle enough."

"I won't be, Mama. I love him and he loves me."

I was pretty sure Joe's thoughts were the same as mine because a little while after we were all done eating the apple nut wedding cake for dessert, Joe said, "Well, folks, if y'all don't mind, I think

Anna's pretty much worn out from all the excitement today, so we're just gonna go on ahead home. Ma, Pa, we'll see you in the morning. Take your time here visitin' and make yourself at home when you decide to go back to our place." I wondered if Papa was going to have to take them home if we took the buggy that Joe and his parents arrived in.

But that thought was fleeting. When I heard Joe say, "our place," that sounded so nice to me...*our* place. I think I knew at that point how Joe must have felt when he first bought Mary's farm.

"Okay, Son," said his Pa with that Southern drawl. "We'll stay on here for a bit and visit. You kids go on." I don't know if I imagined it, but I thought I saw him wink!

So many feelings were going on inside my head and my stomach...excitement, fear, anticipation, love, and of course, those dang butterflies.

Doug and Lonny had taken my things over to Joe's that morning while everyone was getting ready for the day. Mama had sent away for the prettiest nightgown for me to wear our first night together. It was white chiffon, and I'd never slept in anything so lovely. I couldn't wait to wear it for Joe.

When we got outside, I looked around. "Joe, where's your horse and buggy?"

He grinned at me and said, "It's just around the corner. But never mind about that. I want you to close your eyes and stay right here. I got you a wedding gift." He seemed as excited as a little kid on Christmas morning.

Sugarhouse Trials

"Okay, Joe," I said, smiling and laughing, feeling quite giddy. I doubted it was another Bible, but I couldn't imagine what it could be. With my eyes closed, I waited, aware of the quietness of the evening. It was so still and peaceful.

After about five minutes, I could hear him approach. The next sound I heard was a snort, and I couldn't help but open my eyes. Joe was leading the most beautiful white stallion I'd ever seen. He said, "Remember when I was late for Ella's wedding and I told you I had to see a man in Benson about buying an animal?"

"Yes," I said breathlessly. "I remember. I forgot all about it."

"Well Anna, meet Kit. He's all yours. He's been with Buddy learning how to be a gentleman so y'all can ride him safely." Joe was grinning from ear to ear.

"Oh, Joe! I don't know what to say!" I scratched Kit behind the ear. "He's beautiful! Thank you! I'll care for him just like he was my own child!"

Joe handed me an apple. "Here, make friends." Kit took the apple from my hand greedily, nuzzling and nodding at me as if he approved. It was the beginning of a beautiful friendship.

"Come on, Mrs. Fletcher. Let me hitch you up on his back so we can all go home."

Joe climbed on behind me, and we trotted away to our new life.

When we got home, Joe tended to Kit as I readied myself for my wedding night. Mixed emotions flooded my mind and my heart. I wondered if I would please Joe in our marriage bed. I was a naïve virgin who really had no idea of the details in the art of lovemaking. I hoped he would be patient with me. I undressed and carefully donned the chiffon nightgown. It was white with delicate pink-and-blue ribbons woven through at the neckline and wrists. Wearing it made me feel beautiful. I brushed my hair and rinsed my mouth. Mama had given me some rosewater to dab behind my ears, but I also touched the tip of my tongue with it. It was quite nasty tasting, but I was hoping it would make the kissing more enjoyable for Joe. Just as I was placing the cap back on the bottle, Joe entered the room.

If I thought Joe had looked at me like he could eat me up before, *this* look he was giving me was more like he'd devour me.

"Oh, Anna," he breathed. "How did I get so lucky to have you as my own? Do you even know how beautiful you are?" He walked up to me and took my face in his hands. My heart was beating so loudly, I was sure he must be able to hear it. As I looked up at him, he bent down and gave me the most intimate kiss. I was feeling things that I had never felt before, and I liked it.

Very gently, he picked me up and laid me on the bed. I watched as he undressed, and while it was a little uncomfortable and somewhat embarrassing, I couldn't seem to take my eyes off him. He had muscles in his arms that I had never noticed before, and they flexed as he undressed. When he stood before me naked, I whispered, "You are beautiful, too, Joe."

He laughed and said, "Men aren't beautiful, Anna...we're handsome!"

I smiled. "No, Joe; maybe some men are handsome, but YOU are beautiful!"

Sugarhouse Trials

That was a night that was etched in my mind forever. We didn't get much sleep. It was fun and exciting and in those few hours, I really got to know my husband in body and soul.

When I awoke the next morning, he was lying on his stomach, fast asleep with his arm over my belly. My first thought was embarrassment when I remembered what had taken place the previous hours, but as I studied his handsome face, all those warm, loving feelings flooded back to me and I kissed him. Before he even opened his eyes, he smiled, grabbed me, and gave me one of "those" kisses. I thought, *I'm going to love married life!*

PART TWO

CHAPTER NINETEEN

Indeed, married life suited me. Mama was such a good example and teacher; I just fell into being a farmer's wife. Joe was the perfect husband and appreciated everything I did to help run the farm. Cora was such a support to me, and she and I became the best of friends; and Joe and Buddy made a great team, sharing the different chores. I was so proud of the way Joe caught on to farming and sugaring and cider-making so quickly. We had a small apple orchard, and it was one of my jobs to help pick apples when they were ripe in the fall. If Cora was available, I'd take her along with me and we'd visit and laugh and share stories while we picked. One day, I asked her if I could ask a personal question.

"Well, of course, Anna. What is it?"

"Did you *ever* have a beau?"

She looked at me and I could tell she wasn't expecting *that* question. "Ummm...well, yes, actually. His name was Roy Feldman. We courted for about a year."

"What happened? How come you didn't marry him?" She looked sad all of a sudden. "I'm sorry, Cora. That isn't my business. I shouldn't have asked."

"No, it's okay, Anna. I haven't thought about Roy in a very long time. I guess I loved him. Who knows what that kind of love is, anyway…he did ask me to marry him, but I don't know. Buddy has never had a woman interest and I just didn't have the heart to leave him. He took care of me my whole life. I didn't want him to be alone."

I thought to myself, *Wow, I was right. That's why neither of them married.* "Well, Cora, that was mighty unselfish of you. Did Buddy ever know Roy proposed to you?"

"Oh, no! I never told him. Roy just stopped coming around and Buddy never asked why. I thought it was for the best."

Right about that time, I was wishing I had never asked the question in the first place. I was trying to think of something lighthearted to change the mood but couldn't think of anything.

Luckily, I was saved by a kitten, of all things. This little fellow came running into the orchard, right toward Cora. She exclaimed, "Why aren't you the cutest little thing! Where did you come from?"

And I thought, *Heaven!*

*****

Kit was my pride and joy. Every morning I'd take him running, sometimes still in my nightgown, both of us feeling free and wild. But I have to admit I looked forward to nighttime, when I would get Joe all to myself. He was a considerate, gentle lover, and my butterflies never went away when we were together. For three years we were childless, and I was beginning to wonder whether there was something wrong with me. I knew Joe had fathered Daniel, so if there was a problem, it had to be me. Finally, when I was almost twenty, Bernice was born. Mama's mother's name was Bernice, and I knew it would mean a lot to her, me giving her the name. Joe and I had agreed that if it was a boy, he'd name him, but if it was a girl, I could name her. He told me afterward that if we'd had a boy, he would have liked to call him Jack because he always liked that name. At the time, I hoped maybe someday there would be a Jack Fletcher.

Bernice's birth wasn't too difficult, considering she was my first. At my initial shriek, Joe got so nervous that Papa took him to the sugarhouse and fed him lots of cider. Normally, Joe didn't touch the stuff, but I guess he was pretty upset. I was sure he was reliving Mel's horror. Papa later told me Joe finally passed out, and Papa just let him sleep it off in the sugarhouse. Mama was there with me, as well as Ella, and of course the midwife. Her name was Ruth. She was a very gentle, quiet-mannered woman with red hair and freckles. She had assisted Ella with her children, and Ella adored her. Ella's second child was a sweet little boy who didn't have colic, named after his daddy, Lewis, but they called him Lew.

Mama was beside herself that she was about to become a grandmother for the third time. We estimated Bernice was about seven pounds, which was a pretty normal size. Joe was proud and seemed to adore her, but secretly, I thought he was a little disappointed she wasn't a boy. I thought about little Daniel, the baby who had died, and I noticed how Joe looked at Lew whenever we visited. He'd never offered to hold Emma when she was first born but was quick to put his arms out for Lew. When asked, he took Bernice, but in my mind, there seemed to be something missing when he looked at her. I realized later that it wasn't true. It was me who had the problem. *I* felt bad that I didn't give him a son first time around.

Bernice was a chubby baby, didn't have colic, and was pleasing to look at. She had Joe's dark hair and my green eyes. And as she grew, I loved her sweet disposition. She loved her Papa Joe, and he did love her. She would follow him around whenever I let her. She also seemed to love farm life, helping with the chickens and becoming friends with all the animals. We were so happy, and life was blissful.

CHAPTER TWENTY

One day, Joe and I decided to take Bernice to Louisiana to meet her other grandparents. She was now two years old, and we felt she was old enough to make the long trip down south.

Trains were much faster than horses and buggies in 1904, and they now had Pullman cars, which were so much more comfortable for passengers. Joe booked the three of us in first class. I was so excited because not only had I never ridden on a train, but I had never left Vermont. This was going to be quite an adventure for me.

It took us a few days to get to our destination. I had a better appreciation of Elizabeth and Lee's presence at our wedding after they'd traveled by train. I kept thinking, *And we still have to take the long ride home!* I wasn't used to sitting for such long periods.

I found it very interesting as we drove through the different states—how they all had their own beauty. I almost wished we had waited until Bernice was a little older so she could appreciate this trip we were taking. She was very well-behaved for the most part. The motion of the train often made her sleepy, so she slept through a lot of the trip.

We arrived very late on a Sunday evening. The train left us about ten miles from the Fletchers', and we could have stayed and spent the night, but Joe just wanted to get home. I think he was tired and anxious because he seemed irritable when I would ask him questions or when Bernice would fuss. I decided it might be better if I just stayed silent. I know he was looking forward to seeing his brothers and spending time with his family.

As our coachman drove up the long driveway, I felt the old familiar butterflies in my stomach. There were strange trees on either side of the drive, which reminded me of my parents' house. Joe told me these trees were called Southern Magnolia trees and produced the sweetest-smelling flowers you could ever smell. I wished it were lighter out so I could see better. When we got out of the buggy, I stared at the building in front of me. It was huge! "This is a house?" I asked. It had huge pillars and was two stories high. There were two porches...one on the bottom floor and one on the top floor. And I thought The Hermitage was big!

"Yes, ma'am...been in the family for generations. What do you think of it?"

"Why, I've never seen anything like it! How many people live in it?"

"Well, darlin', let's find out. I'll take Bernice and have one of the servants come get our luggage later."

Servants? Guess I'm not in Vermont anymore. Slowly, I eased out and stretched. My legs felt cramped and my back ached. I sure was glad to be able to stand and walk around. Between the train and buggy ride, it had been a long, tiring day.

Someone must have sensed our presence because before we could even get to the top of the stairs, the door flew open. Elizabeth was there with a huge grin on her face. "Thank God you made it here safe and sound. I've been so excited about this visit…let me have that baby girl!" Joe laughed and handed Bernice over to Elizabeth. Bernice was still half asleep, so she just put her head down on Elizabeth's shoulder and closed her eyes. Elizabeth looked like she was in heaven. "Well, come on in, you two!"

Joe teased her, saying, "Oh, so we're invited in, too? Thought for a moment y'all were just gonna steal Bernice and shut the door on us."

"You are a silly boy, Joseph Fletcher…now, come on in. Anna, it's so good to see you again. How was the trip?"

"Tiring," I said, "but interesting. I was telling Joe how much I enjoyed seeing the different states we went through. All of them have their own beauty. We saw the most beautiful horses in Tennessee. Joe told me they were Tennessee walking horses. I think that was my favorite thing to see."

"I agree, Anna. They are beautiful animals. Well, come on. I'll ring Jessie and have her bring some refreshments. We'll go to the sitting room. Do you think we should put Bernice to bed first? As much as I'd love to just sit and hold her, I want her to be comfortable."

Joe said, smiling, "She looks pretty comfortable to me. You can hold her for a while if you want."

"I do want."

"Where's Pa?"

"Oh, he'll be back soon. Some kind of trouble with one of the gins. He and your brother Ethan are having a look at it. Anna, do you need to use the water closet, or is there anything special I can get you?"

"No, Mrs. Fletcher; thank you. I'm good for right now. But if you don't mind, I think I'll stand a bit...I'm not used to sitting so much."

"That's fine, dear. Let me call Jessie."

There was a bell with a rope tied to it, and no sooner did she ring it than a very pretty young black girl appeared in a blue uniform with a white apron. "Yes, ma'am?"

"Jessie, please bring us some refreshments. My son and his family have been traveling all day and they're hungry and thirsty."

"Yes, ma'am...right away, ma'am."

Wow, I thought, *Mama could sure use a Jessie.* Especially now that I wasn't there to help her anymore.

Jessie came in soon after with some sweet tea and a plate of really delicious tiny sandwiches. There were a variety of meats and cheeses as well as fresh fruit and little cakes. I ate until I was full.

Bernice woke up, and when she saw a stranger holding her, she looked alarmed. Her bottom lip stuck out and tears formed in her eyes.

"It's okay, baby girl," I cooed. "This is Gramma Elizabeth. She's Papa's Mama." Bernice turned and looked at Elizabeth, puzzled. I offered her a small cake, and she was happy to get it.

Right about that time, we heard a noise in the foyer, and a loud boisterous voice boomed out, "Are y'all here already?" Lee practically danced into the room, a huge smile on his face. "Anna, Joe! And looky here! Is this Miss Bernice??"

Poor Bernice...it was too much for her, and she started crying. I took her from Elizabeth and told her not to cry. "This is Grampa Lee, Papa's Papa."

Lee was already shaking Joe's hand and apologizing for being so loud. "Didn't mean to scare the itty-bitty."

"She'll be fine," I said. "She's just tired from the trip."

"Sorry I wasn't here to meet y'all," Lee said a bit quieter, "But one of the gins was acting up, and you can't run a business a hundred percent if your machines aren't doing their jobs."

"No problem, Pa. We're planning on staying for a while, so we'll have plenty of time to visit and catch up," replied Joe.

Elizabeth said, "I'm sure you all are very tired right about now. Joseph's right...we'll have more time to catch up tomorrow. Why don't y'all head upstairs? I'll have George get your things and bring them up to you."

"Sounds good to me, Ma. Here, Anna, let me have Bernice. I'll carry her up." Once I gave her over to Joe, Lee gave me one of his bear hugs that crushed my ribs.

"So glad to have ya here, Anna. Hope y'all will enjoy some good Southern hospitality. Anything you want or need, you just ask."

"Thanks, Mr. Fletcher. Right now, I guess the only thing I need is a nice, comfortable bed."

"That you'll have. Joe, we've got y'all in your old bedroom. There's a crib in there for Bernice. Anything else you need, just holler."

"Thanks, Pa. Appreciate it."

Not too long after we had entered the bedroom, there was a knock on our door. When Joe opened it, there was a huge, older black man standing there. "Got your luggage, Mr. Joe," he said.

"George! Good to see you, man...how've ya been?"

"Just fine, Mr. Joe. We've missed ya...how've you been? Congratulations on your new family!"

"Well, George, come on in and meet them! Anna, this is George. He's been with our family for years...ever since I was a young tyke."

"Pleased ta meet ya, Miss Anna. Welcome to Magnolia Hill."

"Magnolia Hill? Why, Joe, you didn't tell me this beautiful home had a name."

"Guess it just slipped my mind, darlin'...and George, this is our little girl, Bernice."

George smiled at her and said, "Aren't you jes the prettiest little girl!" Bernice didn't know what to make of George, so she just stared. "Well, nice to meet ya, Miss Anna...I'll let you folks get settled, but if you need anything at all, y'all be sure to let me know, ya hear?"

"Will do, George; thanks for your help." George bowed and left us. I was so tired, I didn't even look at our surroundings. I

Sugarhouse Trials

slipped my nightgown on, put a nightdress on Bernice, changed her diaper, and fell into bed.

The three of us slept later than we normally would have the next morning. Joe woke first, and his stirring caused me to open my eyes. The first thing I noticed was that the room was a beautiful pale yellow. We were in a very comfortable four-poster bed that was made from a dark reddish-looking wood. It was nothing like our lighter maple furniture in Vermont. Joe told me it was cherry, and I thought it was beautiful. There was an ornate fireplace across from it, and to the side was a huge chest of drawers made of the same cherry wood. The windows in the room were floor-length with heavy velvet drapes the color of rust. I noticed our bedspread was the same color.

Bernice was sound asleep in her crib. She looked like a little angel lying there with her thumb in her mouth, working away at it.

I whispered, "Good morning, Joe." He came to my side and hugged and kissed me.

"Good morning to you. Let me go downstairs and see what's going on. Would you like a cup of coffee?"

"Sounds good…I'd love one." As Joe disappeared from the room, I got out of bed and looked out the window. The grounds were impeccable. Now I could get a better look at those trees. They sure were pretty, and I couldn't wait to get close and smell their aroma.

As I looked further down the way, I saw a couple of black men heading toward what looked to be a livery barn. *These must be more servants hired to help run this huge place,* I thought. I couldn't wait to explore everything. It was so different than Vermont. I wondered why Joe would want to leave all this for a small farm in Vermont.

Joe came back with a coffee for both of us, and we sat and drank it together, waiting for Bernice to wake up. It didn't take long. She opened her eyes and looked around. I was sure she was wondering where the heck she was, but being a curious baby, there were no tears as she looked about. Her eyes found us quick enough, and a big smile appeared. Joe went to her and picked her up, and the three of us headed down the staircase.

I'd always admired Grampa Ev's staircase at The Hermitage, but this one was something to behold. You could go up one side, across the landing, and down the other, like a double staircase. I could imagine Mary's kids having a ball running up, over, down, and back up again. Because I was so tired when we arrived, I hadn't really noticed the beauty of the place. It was nothing like a farmhouse. This was elegant like I would imagine a king's palace to look like. There were many portraits in the bedroom, front room, and dining room. I wanted to study them and get further acquainted with my husband's family because these people were my children's ancestors…past and present.

Joe guided Bernice and me to the dining area, where Elizabeth was seated. It seemed everything in this house was elaborate. All the furniture was fancy and so very different from the country style in Vermont.

Jessie was already setting a variety of breakfast foods on the table. I saw a pitcher of orange juice on the sidebar with coffee, cream, and sugar. On the table were platters of bacon, eggs, cornbread, syrup, and what I was about to learn was hominy.

Elizabeth smiled as we approached. "Good morning! Have a seat, please and help yourself. Lee has already eaten and is back at the mill. He told me to have you join him, Joseph, after you've had something to eat. Your brothers are with him and they can't wait to see you."

"Well, I can't wait to see them either, Ma. I trust you probably have plans for Anna and Bernice?" We sat down at the table, filled our plates, and started to eat. I had a taste of everything, but I think my favorite was the hominy and bacon gravy. I couldn't get enough of it. But I was surprised when I tasted the syrup. It sure wasn't our pure maple syrup.

Elizabeth continued, "Why, as a matter of fact, I do. I thought Anna would enjoy a walk around the gardens, and we'll take Bernice to see the baby animals that were born not too long ago. All children love baby animals."

"Some adults love baby animals, too," I added with a grin.

"Well, good. We have a plan, at least for today. I figure once Bernice gets used to me, you can take Anna and show her Shreveport and I'll have some alone time with this sweet girl."

After we had eaten our fill, Joe went off, and Bernice and I went upstairs to get ready for our adventure. Elizabeth was the perfect guide, showing us all around the gardens, paying special attention to Bernice. She held her hand and pointed out all the pretty flowers. Joe was right about magnolias. They smelled divine.

Bernice was starting to warm up to Gramma Elizabeth. She was infatuated by all she saw and started pointing out the butterflies and birds. At two, she was a smart little girl. She was getting good at saying words, but you had to listen carefully. A couple of times I had to translate for Elizabeth when Bernice said something to her.

Before we knew it, it was time for lunch. It seemed like that was all we'd been doing since we got there…eat, eat, eat. But the food was delicious and different, and I wasn't complaining. There was fried chicken, black-eyed peas, collard greens, and corn pone. The best treat was a pecan pie for dessert. I felt like my clothes were already getting tighter. All five brothers and Lee joined us for the buffet that was set out. It was pretty overwhelming to see the five of them together. They were all tall, strapping men. Ethan, the oldest, looked most like Lee. After Ethan was Jeremiah, who resembled both parents; Brett came next, and he and his brother Boyd looked a lot like Joe. They all gave hugs like their Pa, and it left me out of breath by the last hug. It was amusing to watch them eat and talk all at once. Bernice just stared.

When the men finished eating, Ethan said, "Well this was fun, y'all, but now it's time to get back to the mill." As the brothers were all saying their good-byes and going out the door, Joe looked at me with a question in his eyes.

I knew what he was asking. "Go, Joe…go be with your brothers. I think Bernice and I are going to have a little nap."

"Are ya sure, darlin'?"

"Yes, I'm sure…hurry now." He kissed me, his mother, and Bernice and ran out the door.

"Anna, I want to thank you for bringing my son back to me," Mrs. Fletcher said quietly.

I looked at her quizzically. "What do you mean?" I hoped she didn't mean brought him back to stay.

"Well, after Mel and little Daniel died, Joseph changed. He became a very bitter, angry man. He blamed himself for their deaths and couldn't forgive himself. He started drinking and wouldn't talk to anyone unless it was a grumbly or mean comment. When he decided to go to Vermont, it hurt me deeply because I didn't want to lose him, but Lee talked to me and explained that it would probably be the best for Joseph to start again…have a new beginning and forget about the past. When he met you that first day, do you know he actually sent us a telegram telling us that he'd met his Vermont bride?"

"No, I had no idea. I knew he told me early on that he wanted me to be his wife. It kind of scared me."

"Well, I can imagine why. You were only fourteen at the time, right?"

"Yes, ma'am. But the feelings I had for Joe were nothing like any other feeling I had felt before, so I was sure it was love."

Elizabeth laughed. "Well, Anna, again, thank you. He hasn't been this happy in a very long time. I'm proud to call you daughter."

"Thank you, Mrs. Fletcher."

"You know, you can call me Elizabeth if you want."

"Maybe I'd feel more comfortable with Gramma Elizabeth…if that's okay with you."

"That's fine with me. Is there anything you need before you take this sleepy girl upstairs?" I looked at Bernice and sure enough, she was knocking nails.

"No; everything is perfect. We have everything we need. Thank you, Gramma Elizabeth."

She smiled, and for the first time, I noticed faint dimples in her cheeks. I thought about what she'd said about Joe. Now I understood why he hardly ever accepted Papa's cider or whiskey.

*****

Our time in Louisiana was going fast. We had already been there for two weeks. We had one week to go. I got to meet and spend time with all the brothers' wives. They were all delightful ladies who loved to sit and talk while drinking sweet tea in their gardens. They all had maids and cooks and housekeepers. Even their children had nannies. Life was so different there.

By this time, Bernice was very comfortable with Gramma Elizabeth, as she was with Lee, her uncles, aunts, cousins, and all the servants. Everyone doted on her, and I wondered if we would be bringing home a spoiled child.

Joe took me on a tour of the Louisiana he grew up in. We drove along the Red River, and I was amazed at how much bigger this river was than our own Woods River. I think it was even bigger than the Connecticut River. He showed me where the riverboats docked and where he used to load and unload the cotton when he was married to Mel. We took rides past the swamps, where Joe told me about alligators. They sounded like fierce creatures, and I was glad we didn't have them in West Langford. He showed me a couple of rice plantations as well as the sugarcane fields. It was, as Joe had told me years ago, so very different than Vermont. All in all, it was a learning experience, and again I was wishing Bernice was a little older so she could enjoy all of this and learn of her father's heritage.

Sugarhouse Trials

One night while we were getting ready for bed, I asked Joe, "Do you miss living here, Joe?"

He looked at me long and hard before answering. "Ya know, Anna, the first couple of days, I thought I did. Growing up here was pretty amazing, but pretty soon, I started missing our life back in Vermont. I feel proud of what you and I have accomplished, with the help of Buddy and Cora and your family and all. How about you? Would you like to live here?"

"No way, Joe!" I exclaimed a little too loudly. "Oh, sorry…didn't mean for it to come out like *that*. Your family has been wonderful; the house and grounds are beautiful; the food is delicious. I feel like a spoiled little rich girl because there are no chores for me to do. I think it's a fine vacation, Joe, but I'm eager to get back to our farm."

"Well, I sure am happy ta hear that, darlin', 'cause my father invited us to come here and live with them, and I told him *thanks but no thanks*…in the kindest of words, mind you."

"That was very generous of him, for sure, but I'm glad we both feel the same." I knew if we moved here, I'd become fat and lazy and Bernice would definitely be a spoiled child. It would not be a good life for us. Plus, I'd miss Mama, Papa, and my family.

It was a difficult good-bye for the Fletcher family. I think Elizabeth took it the hardest. I could tell she was struggling to hold back the tears as we hugged our good-byes. She took Bernice's little face in her hands and squished her cheeks. "Don't y'all go forgetting your Gramma Elizabeth, little one. Gramma Elizabeth loves you!" And she kissed those little sweetheart lips. Of course, I got the bear hugs from all the Fletcher men, and again, I had to struggle to catch my breath. Ethan offered to take us to the train station. Once the train started to move, I sighed deeply and was happy to be heading toward home. Joe looked over at me, took my hand, and squeezed it. I was thinking he must be feeling the same way.

The trip north seemed surprisingly shorter than the trip south. It went pretty uneventfully, except for one day when Joe had a confrontation with one of the other passengers. The man was drunk and was talking to me, touching my arm. I tried to move back away from him, but he was persistent. Joe was ready to punch him when I yelled, "No, Joe. Stop!" I surely didn't want to make a scene on the train. Joe pushed him and the man staggered backward, then headed in a different direction.

"Were you flirting with him, Anna?" he asked me angrily.

"No, Joe! All of a sudden he was there in front of me and Bernice. I wouldn't do that; you know me!"

"Well, maybe I don't," he replied grumpily.

Wow, he must be overtired or something, I thought. He frowned and told me he needed to go for a walk. When I started hearing a couple of loud cuss words, people were beginning to stare, so I cuddled Bernice in my arms and began to sing softly to her.

When he finally came back, I assumed he was still angry because he didn't talk for quite a while. After a bit, I got up the nerve to tell him Bernice and I were getting hungry. She was getting whiney, and I couldn't quiet her. He nodded and said he would go see about getting some food.

The rest of the trip went smoothly, and we finally arrived back home late one afternoon. Buddy and Cora were at the train station to take us home, and to our surprise, Mama, Papa, and my brothers were waiting for us, standing around the garden. I was so happy to be home, I practically jumped out of that buggy. I hugged everyone, and there were many questions about our trip. Mama had already grabbed Bernice, and she was hanging on to Mama's neck like there was no tomorrow. Cora had told them we were coming home this day because Joe had sent a telegram to Buddy. Bless her heart, she had made lots of food, so we were all able to sit and eat together and tell everybody about our Louisiana adventure. I wondered if we would be making that same trip the next year.

CHAPTER TWENTY-ONE

Time went on, the days pretty routine—just good, simple farming life. We were all glad to be back home. I felt useful again as I did my chores, often thinking about how very different my life would be if we lived in that huge house with servants. No way would I be happy and fulfilled, and I knew Joe felt the same way.

Every day when my chores were finished, I loved putting Bernice in front of me on Kit's saddle as we rode around town together. Kit was very special to Bernice, and she always helped me tend to him. Sam especially appreciated the visits we would make to his store. He and Freda would spoil Bernice and give her little gifts and candy, making a big fuss over her. Their children were all grown, and while I did know they had grandchildren, it seemed they didn't visit very often. Bernice loved the attention and would often beg me to take her to see "Uncle Sam and Auntie Freda."

Every Sunday, we'd all meet at Mama and Papa's for Sunday dinner. If Joe wasn't able to make it because of a farming problem, Bernice and I would take Kit. Bernice's cousins would stare in awe when we rode into the drive. Kit was a sight to behold. He was a beautiful animal and because Bernice was so small, he looked huge and scary to some of her younger cousins.

Our family was growing. Ella now had three children, and Lonny had married and had two of his own. Finally, one of the many girls who had fancied Lonny got his attention. Her name was Lucy Mae Jenkins. She was around my age and came from a good family in East Langford. She was a tiny little thing, even shorter than me, with long, blonde hair and the biggest blue eyes I'd ever seen. One couldn't help but love her, as she was sweet as honey. I was happy for Lonny and glad that at least one of my brothers was to have a life of his own. Lonny bought a farm in East Langford, not far from Lucy Mae's homestead. I knew Doug missed him a lot, but like me, he loved our brother and was happy for him. Lonny and Lucy Mae wasted no time having babies, and I wondered why Ella and Lonny had both had children so fast and it took me forever to have Bernice. Bernice loved her cousins like they were her own brothers and sisters, and again I wondered why she didn't have a sibling of her own. It wasn't like Joe and I weren't trying. Soon, Bernice would be starting school, and I was itching to hold another babe in my arms.

Season after season, Joe, Buddy, Cora, and I—and now even little Bernice, who was already six years old—worked the farm side by side, making a go of it. Leo started to accept Joe and came by occasionally to help when we needed him, although Joe acted

Sugarhouse Trials

formal and cool around Leo. Because his father and mother were getting up in years, Leo was becoming more responsible for the upkeep of the Decker farm, but he always seemed to have time for us when we needed him. Mostly, it was Buddy who requested Leo's help when Papa needed Buddy. Joe and Buddy reciprocated when Leo needed help, although I sensed Joe wasn't quite as willing as Buddy.

Leo had decided to downsize his farm so he could handle it himself. I used to wonder why Leo hadn't found a nice girl to settle down with. Leo's three older sisters had all married and moved to other towns, so Leo stayed and lived with his Pa and Ma. Cora and I would sometimes bake an extra pie or cake and share it with the Deckers because Leo's Ma had a few medical problems and couldn't stand on her feet for very long. I remember Leo glancing over at me with sad eyes from time to time when he thought I wasn't looking. I hoped Joe would never discover the feelings I now realized Leo really had for me; but deep down, I think he did and that was why he acted the way he did around Leo. It was a weird feeling for me when I finally saw what Lonny probably saw years ago. I was such a naïve girl. Now when Leo looked at me, I realized for him it was anything but an innocent friendship. I now knew that Leo loved me as more than just a friend.

PART THREE

CHAPTER TWENTY-TWO

Life changes can happen overnight. The day our lives changed drastically will be etched in my mind forever. It was summertime. We all had breakfast together very early…about 4:30 a.m., and everyone was in a good mood. Cora often spent the night with us, and Buddy, being such an early riser, was always at our house almost before we were even out of bed. With Buddy and Cora, I felt we were just one big happy family. It was haying season. Like every other previous July, after breakfast, Buddy and Joe went out to harness the horses to the hay mower. Mary had sold Joe her horses, Freddy and Grace, as part of the sale of the farm. Buddy had told me at one point that Grace was a bit skittish, but he said, "She's a young filly, but teaming up with Freddy usually puts her right."

They had been out in the field working about five or six hours when one of our neighbors, John Hood, came riding his buggy into our yard. I was in the garden, sweating in the muggy, stagnant air, picking beans and summer squash. I stood up when I heard him yell, "Anna, Anna!! There's been an accident!"

"What? Who, John? Tell me!!" I felt my stomach drop to my toes.

"It's Joe, Anna! Buddy said the horses got spooked, moved unexpectedly, and Joe's hand got caught in the cutter bar!"

"Oh no!" I shouted. "Is he okay? Where is he?"

"Buddy brought him to your Pa's place, and your father and Doug are on their way taking him to Doc Shepherd's office in Bradford. Your Pa asked me to take you there."

"Okay…yes, John!! Let me tell Cora and I'll be right back." I ran as fast as I could into the house, where I knew Cora and Bernice were baking bread.

Poor Cora. I didn't give her much explanation but told her I had to go to Bradford. "Would you please watch Bernice for me, Cora? I promise I'll explain when I get back home! I've gotta go right now! Joe had an accident and John Hood is taking me to him. I'll give you more details when I get back home."

Cora, being the faithful friend, answered, "Of course, Anna…I'll stay with her for as long as ya need me to." She hugged me and said, "Go! Go!"

Cora, never having children of her own, had a real fondness for Bernice, like she was her own. I wasn't jealous. I felt blessed that someone else loved my little girl as much as I did, and I was grateful to Cora. In fact, Buddy was like another Grampa to Bernice, and I was glad that she always had a very loving family surrounding her.

Sugarhouse Trials

Running toward John's buggy, I jumped into the passenger seat. Even though John was pressing his horse and buggy to maximum speed, I was wishing I was on Kit's back. He'd get me to Bradford a lot quicker than John's filly. My mind was racing, and my heart was beating like a rabbit's. I knew my fingers were fidgeting, but I didn't care. I felt like yelling, "Faster, faster!" I knew John was doing a good thing for me, so, as difficult as it was, I held my tongue. Neither of us said one word the whole way to Bradford. The ride seemed to take forever. My mind was racing so fast, my thoughts were jumbled and didn't make sense. The fear of the unknown is always the scariest kind of fear.

We finally pulled up in front of the doc's house. It was a huge white house, and he had an addition built specifically to see his patients. It was quite different than most houses and was very beautiful. Most doctors, like Doc Shepherd, had their offices right there in their own home. I jumped out and ran to the door with a quick "thanks" to John as I bolted. I pounded on the door, and Mrs. Shepherd opened it. She was a pretty woman with a friendly, sympathetic face, and I liked her immediately. "Please, ma'am...I'm Joe Fletcher's wife, Anna. My Pa brought him here because he hurt his hand."

"Yes, Anna. My husband is with him now. Go down this hall and take a right. You'll see your father and brother in the parlor."

"Thank you so much, Mrs. Shepherd."

I followed her directions, running down the hall and through her kitchen. I spotted Papa and Doug. "Papa! What happened? Is Joe gonna be okay?" It hit me right then, and I burst out crying. Papa came to me and held me in his arms.

"Don't cry, Anna. I'm sure he'll be okay. We got him here as fast as we could. Buddy did good. He wrapped Joe's hand in his shirt and found me and Doug pretty quick. Good ol' Buddy said he would stop at John's house to ask him to bring you here and then he'd go back to your farm to finish the hayin'. Now it's up to the doc to do the rest. Say your prayers, Anna girl."

John came in right about then, and he and Papa were head to head, whispering. I was too upset to care what they were talking about. I started pacing back and forth, wishing I could at least see Joe and let him know I was here. Doug tried to tell me to sit down and try to relax, and I was pretty sure I snapped at him. Looking dejected, he returned to his seat. Doug was a big, gentle giant who had a heart of gold. I often wondered why some girl hadn't snatched him up. He would have made a very fine husband. At that point, however, I wasn't feeling sorry for him. This was my husband in with the doctor, and he was hurt!

Mrs. Shepherd came in a couple of times, asking if she could get us something to drink or eat, but we declined. All our nerves were on edge.

It seemed like hours had gone by when the doctor came out, looking a bit grim.

Papa asked, "How is he?"

"He's pretty out of it right now. You can see him in a minute. He lost a lot of blood, but that's the least of his problems. I'm so sorry to say I believe he'll never have the use of that right hand again. It got pretty mangled, and there wasn't much I could do to save it. I'm so sorry."

Sugarhouse Trials

Sadly, John expressed his apologies, said his good-byes, and told us he had to get back home. Doug said he was going to take the ride back with John so he could get back to work. Sullenly, I gave them both a hug and thanked John for coming to get me. "You are a good neighbor, John. I'm indebted to you."

"No need, Anna; Joe woulda done the same for me if things was turned around."

My eyes filled with tears as I nodded. As I watched him walk out of the room, I selfishly wished things *were* turned around.

Papa finished speaking with the doctor and asked, "You ready to go see Joe, Anna?"

"Yes, Papa."

"Try to be brave, my girl...for Joe."

"Okay, Papa. I'll try."

The two of us entered the stuffy, medicine-smelling room. Joe lay there on a single bed with his hand all bandaged up, looking totally helpless. His eyes were closed, and he looked peaceful, although I had a feeling that when the medication wore off, he would be in a lot of pain. There was a window in the room, but the shutters were closed, so the room was pretty dark.

"Joe, can ya hear me, honey?"

He slowly opened his eyes and tried to focus. "Anna? That you, darlin'?"

"Yeah, Joe. Me and Pa. How ya feeling?"

"Really sleepy. It's hard keeping my eyes open. What happened, anyway? I can't remember much of anything."

Papa took over and said, "You had an accident, Joe. Buddy said the horses got spooked by something and your hand got caught up in the cutter bar."

"Dang, really? How come I don't remember any of that? Am I gonna be okay?"

The two of us kind of looked at each other as if to say, "What do we tell him?"

Papa took the reins and said, "Right now, Joe, all you need to do is go back to sleep and rest for the night. Doc thought it'd be best if you stayed the night here so he can keep an eye on you. I'll bring Anna back in the morning, and if all is well, we'll take you on home."

Joe agreed. "Yeah," he slurred, "sounds good ta me, y'all. Anna, come on over here and give me my good-night kiss."

Papa went to find the doctor before we headed home to get a little more information. Doctor Shepherd had told Papa he was going to write down some instructions on how to treat Joe's hand once we got home. While we were heading home, he told me everything that the doc had told him. Trying not to cry, I asked Papa…"What does this all mean for Joe and our farm, Papa?"

"Well, I don't rightly know. Let's not worry about it tonight. Let's all get a good night's sleep and we'll deal with it tomorrow." I had the feeling Papa was sparing me some very negative thoughts, but he knew how upset I was, so he didn't tell me what he was really thinking.

Bernice and Cora bombarded me with questions when Papa dropped me off home. I just wanted to retreat to my bedroom, but I knew that wouldn't be fair, especially to Bernice. So, I explained to my little girl as much as I knew she could comprehend. I told her Papa had an accident and hurt his hand. He was gonna be okay and she shouldn't worry her pretty little head. "Time for bed, sweetness," I told her with as much comfort as I could muster. Once I got her tucked into bed, I asked Cora to come outside on the porch with me.

"It seems bad, Cora," I confided to her, tears swelling in my eyes. "The doctor told Papa that Joe wouldn't ever have use of his right hand again. He lost two of his fingers and part of his thumb. And what's left of his thumb is useless because of all the nerve damage."

"Oh, Anna, I'm so sorry...does he know yet?"

"No, Papa thought it would be best to tell him tomorrow. Cora, I'm scared. I **know** Joe. He's not gonna be able to run this farm, and I'm not sure he'll be able to deal with that. Buddy's getting on in years, so we can't depend totally on him. I don't know what we're gonna do!!" My emotions were all gloom and doom, thinking the worst.

Cora was silent. I was glad she didn't say an untruth to try and make me feel better. She just sat there and pretty soon took my hand, kinda like the same way I took Joe's hand when he told me about Mel and his baby.

As emotionally and physically tired as I was that night, I hardly slept.

CHAPTER TWENTY-THREE

The next day, as Papa promised, he took me to Bradford. When we entered the room that the Doc had put Joe in for the night, Joe was sitting up, looking off into space at nothing.

"Hey, Joe," Papa said cautiously. "How you doin' today?"

Joe glared—at **me**—and said, "Oh, I'm just fine and dandy, Elmer, for a worthless son of a bitch!!"

My insides felt like something died.

"What do you mean, Joe?" asked Papa. I think he was as shocked as I was by this outburst.

"Well, the Doc told me I would never have use of my right hand again!! How's a farmer supposed to run a farm if he ain't got use of his hands??!! Tell me THAT, Elmer!!" Again, he was looking at **me** like it was **my** fault!

I was so shaken up by the way he was looking at me that I was shocked into silence, wide-eyed and scared to death.

Right then, the doctor came into the room. I could tell he was uncomfortable, and I wondered if Joe had lit into him when he told Joe what was what. "Well, Joe," he said with a heavy sigh, "you can go on home with your family now. I want you to stop at the apothecary and get the medicine I prescribed for you. It'll help with the pain."

"Yeah; okay, Doc. *That'll* help," he said as he rolled his eyes.

The ride home was not very pleasant. I sat in the middle of Papa and Joe and was reminded of the buggy trip with Joe and Leo going to Mary's that first time…how I was trying not to bang into Joe. Well, here I was again, trying not to bang into this tall, dark stranger. And *this* man *was* a stranger. If I thought I was uncomfortable that other time, it was nothing like I was feeling now. How can a person change so quickly? It scared me badly. I kinda leaned toward Papa for a minute, and he put his head down on mine for a split second. I felt his concern and support.

Papa stayed for a bit when we got home, bless his heart. He was trying to lift Joe's spirits, but Joe wasn't having it. Papa finally left, gave me a hug, and whispered, "You need to be strong for him, Anna girl."

I hugged him back but said no words. I wanted him to stay because I didn't know how to act with this angry Joe. I was afraid.

Knowing how much Joe loved good food, I asked him what he wanted to eat. "How 'bout some fried chicken, Joe?" I asked with my best fake smile.

"I ain't hungry, Anna. Just leave me alone for a while."

Bad timing on her part, Bernice bounded into the room. "Papa!!" she exclaimed. "You're home! I missed you so much!!"

Sugarhouse Trials

She ran up to him for hugs and when he pushed her away and I saw her little face crumble, my heart just about broke.

"Not now, Bernice!" he barked. "Go on with your Mama. I need ta be alone right now!"

"Come on, baby; let's go give Kit an apple and a pet." Because Bernice loved Kit almost as much as I did, the distraction worked. Confused and teary-eyed, she looked at Joe and took my hand. I tried to explain how her Papa wasn't feeling all that well right now and that he was tired and grouchy. She knew tired and grouchy. Being farmers, we all experienced that feeling more often than not, but not to this extreme.

Later that evening, after I got Bernice tucked in, I got up the nerve to seek Joe out since he had disappeared and didn't even have supper with us. Buddy popped in on his way home and told me he tried to talk to Joe, but Joe told him he needed to be alone. "Let me know if I can be of help, Anna."

"Thanks, Buddy; I sure will."

Since I knew he wasn't in the house, I looked in the barn first. "Joe, you in here?" No response. I didn't trust that he would respond to me, so I looked all around the barn, cows mooing, the horses snorting at me. Kit nickered, probably thinking I was there with another apple or carrot. "Sorry, you," I said, caressing his nose, "I'll see you later."

The next place I decided to search was the sugarhouse. I probably should have checked there first, as it was one of Joe's favorite places—sugaring was something he really enjoyed. Since sugaring starts in the spring, the sugarhouse hadn't had much activity in months. I was thinking it would be a good hiding place for him.

I hesitated before entering. Who was this stranger who inhabited my husband's body? He scared the heck out of me, and I didn't know how to act with him. I got my wits together and called out, "Joe? You in here?" It was kind of dark, and I couldn't see much. I heard what sounded like a grunt or a growl and followed the sound. Joe was sitting on the floor leaning against the far wall with a whiskey bottle beside him. The bottle was more than three quarters gone. "Joe? You okay?"

"Damn, woman! No, I'm not *OKAY!*"

I shuddered at his tone and sat down beside him. "Oh, Joe, I'm so sorry. What do you want me to do?"

He slurred his words as he said, "Nothin', Anna…I don't need y'all to do nothin'. Just go on and let me be."

"Please Joe…just let me in…don't be like this, please!"

"Be like what, Anna? A broken man who can't do nothin' because he's crippled? I know Leo wants you," he slurred. "I see the way he looks at you…just go on over to him. He can take better care of you and Bernice than I can."

"Joe, you're not thinking straight! I don't want Leo. *You're* my husband. I want you!"

Joe looked at me, half-cocked with a crooked smile, and said, "Anna, honey, I can't even hold ya like a real man anymore. Now go on and get out and just let me be."

I was so hurt and confused. I felt for the first time that nothing in life could stay perfect, and there was nothing absolute in this world. Anything—at any time—could change your life. I stumbled back through the yard and into the house, falling on my bed. I cried myself to sleep and dreamt unsettling dreams.

CHAPTER TWENTY-FOUR

Joe drank every day from then on, starting early in the morning. I knew now what his mother meant when she said Joe was in his "dark time" after Mel and Daniel died. He spent most of his time in the barn or in the sugarhouse. I had no idea what he did in there, and truthfully, I didn't care. Bernice and I both tried our best to avoid him. Buddy was trying to hold everything together, but it was a bit much for a sixty-year-old.

Summer was gone and fall was upon us. I decided to take it upon myself to hire help for Buddy since Joe was refusing to do anything. Cora told me that there was a young fellow who just moved into town with his new wife. His name was Otis Hansen, and his wife's name was Wilma. She said they were living in the cottage at Hood's farm and he was looking for work. Otis had a little experience, as his daddy had a farm in Benton, but apparently, he had a falling out with his parents and so he moved here to West

Langford. I was pretty desperate, so I went to the Hoods' to meet him.

"Hey, Mrs. Fletcher. John Hood tole me ya was looking for help around your farm. I got experience, ya know, and I'm looking for work. I'd be happy ta help ya around yer farm."

I really didn't like his looks or the slowness of his voice and especially the way he was staring at me, but I said, "Well, as a matter of fact, I do need a little help, but it would only be in the fields. I wouldn't want you coming around the house at all. My husband isn't feeling well. I'll have my farmhand, Buddy, get in touch with you. He'll give you direction."

"All right then. Thanks, Mrs. Fletcher. I appreciate this, ya know."

Although I didn't consult Joe, I did ask Buddy *his* opinion. Buddy sighed a long, heavy, defeated sigh and said, "Anna, I am so sorry about everything that's been happening around here. I wish I were ten years younger so I could be more help to you."

"Oh, Buddy, you *are* a help! I don't know *what* Joe and I would've done without you all these years. I just don't know **what** to do. Joe's drunk all the time and I feel like everything is on my shoulders. I don't want to get Papa involved. He's goin' on seventy and can hardly handle his own farm. Luckily, he's got Doug, but with Lonny gone and married, there's only the two of them. I just don't know what to do!" I hiccuped a sob.

Buddy's eyes were filled with sadness. "I think you have no other choice, Anna. You need to hire someone who can help. Don't know much about this feller, Otis, but I guess you gotta give him a try. I'll go talk to him tomorrow."

"Thanks, Buddy. I appreciate that."

I wish I had known a little bit more about Otis before I hired him. I learned much later on that the reason he had a falling out with his parents was because he was a liar and a thief. He stole a lot of money from them by lying to the bank where his father did his business. Rather than press charges, the family kicked him out and told him they never wanted to see him again. He was now dead to them. Of course, Buddy and I had no idea of this information; otherwise, Buddy would never have allowed him anywhere near the farm.

I didn't have much interaction with Otis since I told Buddy to make sure he only worked in the orchard and the fields. Buddy and I both decided it would probably be best if we kept the hiring of Otis from Joe for a while.

CHAPTER TWENTY-FIVE

One of the worst days of my life was the day Joe found out I hired Otis. It was a Monday, and I was hanging our laundry out to dry. Cora had taken Bernice to school and then she was off to help Mama with her laundry. Buddy and I had managed to keep Otis a secret for about three months. Buddy had warned him about staying away from the house, and if Otis had ears, he would've heard around town what a mean son of a bitch Joe was and would be smart to take heed. Buddy was taking care of the work closer to the house, where Joe spent most of his days. Joe always thought of Buddy as a father figure, so he tolerated him, and as far as I knew, he never disrespected Buddy.

I'm not sure why Joe decided to go to the apple orchard that day in September, where he met Otis for the first time. I heard him before I saw him, and he was snarling like a wild dog. I looked up and saw him coming toward me fast with venom in his eyes. "You bitch! What gave you the right to go behind my back and hire another hand?! You think I'm that pitiful that I can't even make any decisions around here anymore?!" With that, he hauled off and belted me with his stub. I was horror-struck and put my hand up to my cheek, not quite comprehending what had just happened. I couldn't say a word. I ran to the barn and without even saddling Kit up, I got on his back and rode hard, not in the direction of Pa and Ma's, but toward Leo's farm. I had no idea where I was riding to; I just knew I had to get away. As I passed Leo's place, he was in his garden, and I saw him look up. He waved, but I didn't wave back. I turned away so he couldn't see my tears. I just rode Kit until I could feel him getting tired. I ended up at the deserted Grange Hall. The Woods River ran behind it, so I led Kit over for a drink. I slumped down on the ground next to him and sobbed. I was feeling very sorry for myself, for Bernice, my parents, and for the whole way life had let me down. I sat there for a while and then I heard, "Anna? Anna? Where are you? I know you're here." It was Leo.

I thought, *He must have jumped on his horse and followed me.* I heard his footsteps approaching. "Go away, Leo...I'm okay," I said, trying to sound normal. "Just need to be alone for a bit."

He stepped around the building and stood quietly behind me. The sound of the river rippling was the only thing I heard.

"Anna, look at me," he said gently.

Slowly, I turned around. I knew my face had already swelled. I could feel the tightness.

"Oh my God, Anna! What happened to you? It was *him*, wasn't it? I'm gonna kill him!"

Sugarhouse Trials

"Stop, Leo! He's hurting and can't deal with it all. He's just frustrated, and he took it out on me because I'm there."

"No, Anna. That's no excuse. Has he done this *before*?" I shook my head and looked back down at the river. I felt so heavy, like there was a huge rock sitting on my heart.

"I knew there was something really wrong. That's why I followed you. Let me take you back to my house so I can tend to that bruise. I have a feeling you may even get a shiner out of that deal." He shook his head sadly and helped me up. "Come on, Anna." His voice was heavy and despondent. He helped me get back on Kit, and the two of us rode slowly and silently back to Leo's farm. Once there, I explained to him how things at the farm were getting behind and how I hired Otis behind Joe's back to help Buddy, and how he thought I was being disrespectful of his ability to run the farm on his own. I'm not sure if Leo knew the extent of Joe's drinking, but I didn't mention it.

Leo said, "I heard that the Hoods had a couple living in their guesthouse and that Buddy had the fellow helping out, but don't know much else about them. If ya want, I can come and help Buddy when he needs it."

I refused, thanking him. I knew that Leo's presence would only make Joe's moods worse. It was an uncomfortable situation for both me and Leo. So, I said, "I'd better be getting back now…Bernice will be home from school soon and will be wondering where I am."

Leo boosted me up on Kit, looked at me with sad eyes, and said, "If you ever need me, Anna…" My eyes teared up, and I turned to ride back home.

CHAPTER TWENTY-SIX

Now that Joe knew about Otis, Buddy had him helping closer to the house. In the following days, Leo made his acquaintance with Otis without my knowing. Leo told Otis and Buddy to keep an eye on me and to report any "accidents" I may have.

After that horrible day, Joe never mentioned Otis's working for us again. I often wondered if Buddy had words with Joe about the hiring of Otis, or if Leo told Buddy about my bruised cheek. I never saw Buddy on a daily basis anymore. He was always busy working and wouldn't necessarily have seen my bruises. Sadly, after Joe's accident, Buddy stopped coming around for meals.

With Otis working in the outbuildings now, he and I sort of became acquainted. I kind of got the impression he was a little backward, but as long as he got some direction from Buddy, he got his work done every day. Kind of strange-looking, he was short of stature with a large head and a round body. His dark-blond hair was on the curly side, and it seemed to me, observing his arms, that he must have sprouted hair all over his body like a bear. I doubted he had had much education because it seemed he ended most of his sentences with, "ya know." His wife, Wilma, came around once in a while to visit and share recipes. They were a very similar couple in many ways, physically and mentally. She was also small and round with dark-blonde, curly hair. I'm sure people could have mistaken them for brother and sister. To my knowledge, they never had children, and I wondered if maybe there was also something physically wrong with one or both of them.

I learned from Wilma that she came from a very poor family. "My Ma died when I was eleven, and my Pa expected me to take over *all* of Mama's duties." She looked over at me nervously as she said this, and I knew what she meant by that. I'd heard of men taking advantage of their own daughters and couldn't even imagine it. My Papa would never even think of doing something so vile. I felt bad for Wilma. She explained, "I met Otis at a store in Benton last year. We started to meet every week, and before I knew it, Otis talked me into marrying him and running away together. We was both escaping our parents." She said Otis had told her his parents were falsely accusing him of something he didn't do. He just wanted to get as far away from them as he could. She thought it was a dream come true that somebody wanted to take her away from the clutches of her abusive father.

The good thing about Wilma was that she never mentioned the bruises I sometimes greeted her with. I was glad of it, so I didn't have to make lame excuses. I wondered if maybe she had suffered the same fate with her horrible father.

Sugarhouse Trials

It seemed Joe had gotten a taste for brutality and got his kicks out of hitting me whenever I annoyed him. I did my best to hide it from everyone, and I think because they knew it was embarrassing for me, no one spoke about it.

In time, it seemed like most people had lost their respect for Joe. Whenever people would come around or Joe went anywhere, he was rude and mean-spirited. I was sure that as I tried to hide the bruises, it was pretty obvious that I took the brunt of his anger and frustrations.

Joe had refused to let me go anywhere by myself. The worst hurt was that he wouldn't let me see my parents. There were no more Sunday, visits and I missed them. One day, we went to Sam's store together. I begged Joe to let me go to the store this one time because I needed some kitchen supplies. Normally Joe would send Cora, but she had to go to Bradford with Buddy for personal reasons. After much pleading, he consented. Of course, he wouldn't let me go alone, so the two of us climbed into the buggy and took a very silent, uncomfortable ride together. Sam sat there on the steps of his store, smoking his pipe. When we pulled up to the store, he nodded at Joe, looked me over quickly from head to toe, concern written all over his face, and asked, "Anna, how've you been? I haven't seen you in quite a while. You okay? Need anything? Anything at all?"

I thought to myself, *Uh-oh, doesn't seem like he's asking me about supplies I might need.* Sure enough, Joe also picked up on it.

"What is it, Sam, that you *think* Anna needs?" he growled in his nasty voice. Sam looked uncomfortable. He glanced at me for help.

"Joe, let it alone. Sam meant nothing by it. Let's just go get our supplies." I got "the look" but because Sam was right there, I didn't get the swat that I would've gotten if we had been alone.

Sam followed us into the store, and I could tell he was watching to see if he could talk to me alone. Joe was too shrewd for that and made sure I was by his side the whole time. I glanced over at Sam, and the look in his eyes was nothing but sadness and pity for me. I didn't like it one bit.

I knew Papa and Mama were aware of what was goin' on, but they never said a word. After the accident, the two of them would come calling on a regular basis, but one day, Joe blew up at them and told them to stay away. He said we didn't need help from them anymore. I knew it was because he felt guilty, and seeing my parents made him feel worse. I'm sure my parents were deeply hurt, but they didn't want to start any trouble, and knowing them, they probably figured this wasn't their business. Buddy and Cora also knew what was going on, but it was an awkward situation, them being our hired help and all. Otis did tell me once that Buddy warned Joe about hurting me…not that it did any good. Said Buddy told Joe he wouldn't even stay around if it weren't for me.

At least Bernice was allowed to go visit my parents. I'd send her with Cora in the summertime on laundry day or with Wilma on a Saturday, along with an apple cake or cobbler. I would purposely make two of each with Mama, Papa, and Doug in mind. I'm sure she was a comfort to them and them to her. One time, she asked me if she could go live with them. I burst into tears and she hugged me and cried, "I'm sorry, Mama…I didn't mean it…I wouldn't

Sugarhouse Trials

leave you." I couldn't talk, but if I were truthful, I would have admitted to her that I wanted to go live with them, too.

After Otis had been with us for a year or so, I noticed he sort of developed a crush on me. I saw that he would often stare at me like a lovesick puppy, and he also started bad-mouthing Joe a lot. Unfortunately, Joe also noticed the attention Otis was paying to me. More than once, I got slapped and called a whore even though I never even had thoughts about being with Otis. I was also accused of having improper relations with Leo, whom I hadn't even seen in a couple of months. Life was becoming unbearable.

Joe was still drinking heavily, and he was such a mean drunk. Bernice no longer idolized him. Rather, when she saw him coming, she ran and hid. We had no visitors and we didn't go anywhere. Ella's husband, Lewis, tried to come and reason with Joe once but had no luck. Lewis was told to "go home and mind your own business!" I saw the look on his face, shaking his head at me as he went out the door, and I felt bad for him because he had lost a friend. My brothers also tried to talk to Joe, but like my parents, they were told to just "leave us alone and don't come back."

CHAPTER TWENTY-SEVEN

One late October night, Otis talked me into going to a Halloween festivity in Woods River. Joe had passed out in the parlor, and I hadn't been anywhere in such a long time. My face was clear of his brutal marks at the time, and Cora was at the house to watch Bernice. I did think of what Wilma would think or say about me going out with her husband, but I guess I didn't care at that point. I was still young and wanted to have some fun for a change. My selfish side told me I deserved it. As we rode to the dance, I told Otis, "Just because I'm going with you to this dance, don't get any ideas that we're courting or that I have eyes for you. Joe would probably kill us both in a heartbeat." I saw the way he looked at me all the time and it gave me the creeps.

"I'd like to kill *him*," Otis mumbled angrily.

I couldn't help but think, *Well, so would I...but that's not gonna happen.*

Lenore Sylvain Dexter

I was surprised at how many people were at the dance. I totally ignored the rude stares as Otis and I walked through the door. I just hoped word wouldn't get back to Joe that I had come with Otis. The music was lively, the cider was plentiful, and everyone looked to be having a great time. I noticed Leo over in a corner with a couple of the neighboring farmers, smoking cigarettes, looking very intent on whatever they were discussing. I walked on over to them, and Leo's eyes got big.

"Anna, what are you doing here? Are you okay?"

"I'm fine," I replied. "I came over with Otis so I could get a little break is all."

"Does **he** know you're here?"

I pulled Leo away from his friends after nodding hello to them. "No, he's been drinking heavily all day. When I left, he was passed out on the couch in the parlor. I'm sure he'll be out for the night, I hope."

"Well, let's get you some cider and set a spell. We haven't talked in a bit."

"I know," I said. "It's so good to see you, Leo."

"Well, Anna, you *know* how I feel about you. I just wish things could be different is all."

"True. So do I. Life is strange the way it all turns out. One minute things are good, and the next, life changes and it all goes to hell."

"Well, I'm just glad you're here." Turning, he asked, "What's up with Otis?" I followed his gaze and saw Otis glaring at us.

Sugarhouse Trials

"Oh, boy…we'd better invite Otis over here to visit with us. I don't want him gettin' ideas about me and you, Leo. He might tell Joe."

"Sure, I'll get us all some cider and tell him to join us. Go sit at that corner table over there."

"Okay; thanks, Leo."

The rest of the night was the most fun I'd had in a long time. I danced with both Leo and Otis, and it felt good to let go and feel free. Leo followed us home when the festivities were over. Otis went on to his wife, but Leo insisted he wait outside until he was sure I was safe in my bed and that Joe was still passed out. I did peek in the parlor before climbing the stairs to my bedroom, and Joe was still in the same position I'd left him in. I checked in on Bernice and she was curled up with Cora, who was snoring gently. I'm not sure how long Leo waited outside because my head hit the pillow and I was out.

CHAPTER TWENTY-EIGHT

Months dragged on. The farm was holding on okay, and at least we weren't in the hole. Buddy was able to fix the major repairs with the help of Otis, but the farm didn't look quite as fresh as before the accident. It made me sad because I grew up on a farm that was picture-perfect. Life on a farm isn't the most exciting. Day after day, you get up, do your chores, eat, and go to bed, then you wake up the next morning and repeat what you did the day before. I often wondered how long I would last in this sad routine. When I was working beside Joe, it had meaning. Now, I just went through the motions by myself. I was lonely. Many times, I would daydream of taking Bernice and Kit and we would just ride and ride til we were far away...somewhere where it was bright and happy. But Mama and Papa had instilled in us kids never to be quitters, so I knew I would never do it.

I was in charge of the finance books now. I was surprised Joe trusted me with them. At first, he did them himself, but when he started drinking so much, he made many mistakes. The bank came to visit us one day, and that's when Joe reluctantly handed them over to me. I thought of when I was younger, sitting in Papa's office in that big comfy chair, watching him with his head down, concentrating. Now here I was, doing what the man of the house should be responsible for. I guessed I should have been thankful that at least I was born with enough brains to do it, but I was becoming good at self-pity. I just wished I had my old Joe back. We were barely making ends meet about this time. Buddy and Cora insisted that their paychecks decrease a little so as to help. As much as it pained me to do it, I had no choice. Buddy must have mentioned something to Papa because he told Buddy to tell me that I could count on him and Mama to help out. I knew they probably could afford to help me, but my pride stepped in the way and I just couldn't ask them. Nevertheless, I guessed I was a pretty good money manager because we were never in the red when I managed the books.

Things continued on the same for a few years. It had been almost three years since Joe's accident. The beatings still came, but not quite as often. Otis, one day, confessed his undying love for me, and I just laughed and made out like he was just joking with me. Joe watched the two of us closely, and I knew that in his head, Otis and I *must* be having an affair. Depending on his mood or how much he'd had to drink that particular day or night, that determined my fate. Joe and I hadn't been "together" in years. In fact, he hadn't even walked into our bedroom since Papa and I brought him home from Doc Shepherd's house the day after the

Sugarhouse Trials

accident. Sometimes I really missed being held and loved, but I certainly did not want that from Otis!

One frosty winter day, Leo came by to make sure we had enough firewood in the woodshed. Every year in late summer or fall, everyone would cut wood for the following year because it had to be dry before we could burn it, and then we would fill our woodshed with the chopped firewood we had cut the year before. Leo knew we were short-handed, and I appreciated his concern.

It was January, and the whole northeast was having a deep freeze. It sure didn't help Joe's mood any when we lost most of our apple trees that winter. We relied on our apples for not only cider, which was *his* biggest concern, but for desserts like apple pan dowdy and pies, food for the pigs, and treats…not only for us, but for the horses, too.

That winter was so cold that the Woods River actually froze up and kids thought it was something to be able to walk across it.

Otis was also at the woodshed when Leo came by, and the three of us were chatting together and laughing, innocent enough, huddled together outside the woodshed trying to keep warm. Joe just happened to step out of the sugarhouse (his favorite hideaway) and spotted us. He staggered, narrowed his eyes, and turned around and went back in. Both Leo and Otis looked at me in concern.

"Guess you two better get on out of here," I muttered. "He doesn't look so happy."

"Is Cora still with you?" asked Leo.

"Yes. Don't worry so much."

Otis said, "I hate that son 'a bitch!"

"Go on, now. I'll be fine," I lied. I knew better, but I didn't want them to start something bad.

That evening, after Cora and I cleaned up the supper dishes, Joe, drunk as usual, growled at Cora. "Go upstairs with Bernice and don't y'all come back down tonight. Ya hear me?" Cora looked at me with scared eyes, but she never disobeyed Joe. She saw what happened when I made him mad, and she wanted no part of that. I was surprised and so thankful she stayed with me most nights, helping me care for and watch over Bernice.

"Good night, Anna. See you in the morning. Bernice, go on over and give your Mama a kiss good night. We'll read a bedtime story together." Just as I had, Bernice was going to Miss Everdeen's school and loved reading books.

"Okay, Miss Cora," she said, looking warily at Joe. I took her in my arms and gave her a big hug.

"Love ya, baby girl. Sleep tight. Don't let the bedbugs bite."

"Love you too, Mama. See you in the morning. Do you think we can take Kit for a ride to see Leo tomorrow?" I cringed inside, thinking that was not a good thing for Joe to be hearing right now. We usually snuck over to Leo's when Joe was wasted. Bernice was supposed to keep those visits a secret.

"We'll see, Bernice. Now scoot!"

Joe waited until he heard their bedroom door close before he turned on me. Slurring his words, he asked, "So, now you're turning my own daughter away from me? I seen the way she looks at me, all scared and all. You take her to Leo's behind my back often? Does she call *him* Papa?" He let out a very loud, disgusting burp. Joe had let himself go. Instead of the tall, dark, handsome man who used to be my husband, this man looked like a drunken bum. And because he hardly bathed anymore, he stank.

I tried not to let the disgust show in my face. "Don't be silly, Joe. She just likes to go there 'cause he gives her as much maple sugar on snow as she wants. He spoils her since he doesn't have kids of his own."

"Yeah, right...I still think y'all got something goin' on with him, and Otis, too! I know how much you like it in bed, you whore! So tonite, *darlin'*, I'm gonna remind you how it is with a *real man*, just in case you forgot." With that said, he stood before me, pulled me by the hair into the parlor, and tried to lay me down on the couch. Not wanting Bernice or Cora to hear what was going on, I fought him silently. He was so strong, and his breath reeked of stale whiskey. Even with his impaired right hand, he was able to control me.

I wanted to scream. I was crying and pleading with him... "Please, no! Joe, please stop!"

"Shut up, bitch!" He hit me hard on the side of my head, and I blacked out for a while. When I came to, my dress was hiked up and he was having his way with me. I had given up fighting, feeling defeated, lost, defiled, and dead inside. I cried silently, waiting for it to be over. What had happened to my considerate, gentle Joe? That made me cry all the more for the loss I was feeling. This was NOT the man I married. This was some stranger who inhabited Joe's body. I hated this man, and now I felt little shame for wishing he were dead and gone from our lives.

CHAPTER TWENTY-NINE

After Joe was "done" with me, he passed out. I slid out from under him and slowly, painfully made my way up the stairs to my bedroom. What I wanted to do was fill the washtub and take a bath to cleanse myself, but it was late and dark, and I didn't have the energy. I undressed and pulled my flannel nightgown over my head. As I lay in bed, I fantasized about ways I could get rid of the monster who lived with us in this house. But I knew I could ever do anything like that. It wasn't in my nature.

The next day, while I was out in the barn combing Kit, Otis came down from the loft with some hay. When he saw me, he could tell I'd had a rough night. I had a bruise on the left side of my head from my eye down to my chin, and surely my face said it all. I had cried most of the night, so I could feel that my eyes were red and my face puffy.

"Hey, Anna." He stared at me with wide eyes. "Oh my God! You doin' okay?" he asked in his slow, simpleminded way.

"Yeah, Otis, just fine and dandy," I replied sarcastically.

"I knew he was gonna do something when he saw the three of us out by the woodshed yesterday! Anna, if you ever want me to help you…ya know, get rid of him…I would do that for you, ya know? We could run away and live in New Hampshire and nobody would find us. I got relatives there we could stay with."

Unable to help myself, I laughed, trying to control it so I wouldn't go into hysterics. "Oh, Otis, you are something! No way. We could never get away with that. You have Wilma…I have Bernice…no way. I don't want to run away to New Hampshire. I don't need that kind of help from you right now…so come on, be *real*, Otis! Go on back to your chores. That's what I need you to do right now."

"Well, I'm just sayin'…there are ways to make it look like an accident or suicide. You know my feelings for ya, Anna. I'd leave Wilma in a second if you wanted me to, ya know."

"No, Otis, I DON'T want that. It'll all be okay; don't you worry. Just do what you're hired to do here and leave it alone!"

We didn't speak of it again for some time. Otis hated Joe but liked Buddy, so he did his chores the best as he was able. I continued to live in hell, but the farm continued to survive. Things got worse for me. Joe decided that he could and would take me whenever he wanted. So it was not only the beatings now, but constant rape on top of everything else. I tried fighting back, but it only seemed to make him more violent. I knew it was all about his insecurities. He felt weak and useless. I also knew it made him feel

Sugarhouse Trials

better being able to have some kind of physical control over me. I was at my breaking point. I hated myself for considering the offer Otis had made to me. Maybe we *could* get away with it. Joe had so many problems, people *might* believe he would commit suicide.

I went to Leo and asked him to help me refresh my ability to shoot a rifle. Papa had shown me how to use one when I was just a young girl, but that was a long time ago and I needed a brush-up. Joe had a rifle, which he hadn't used since the accident. I took it to Leo's house. He cleaned it and inspected it, put bullets in it, and said, "Come on, Anna. I'll teach you how to defend yourself if need be." Leo probably would have spit if he knew what I was really thinking. His sweet Anna would never even think about committing out-and-out murder. He was thinking of self-defense. Bad Anna was thinking of survival for myself and my little girl. As he set the targets up on the tree stumps in his back field, I imagined Joe's head as I aimed at the cans.

It was a very long, cold winter. I tried to keep my spirits up for Bernice, but it wasn't easy. Surprisingly, I talked Joe into letting Bernice get a horse for Christmas. She loved animals like I did, especially Kit, and I thought having a horse of her own would distract her from her horrible family life and teach her responsibility. I also thought it would be fun to go riding together when Joe wasn't around. Buddy offered to find her a pony. He had a good friend who bred horses and because he was a friend, he gave Buddy a good price on a small, docile, well-mannered mare for Bernice. I was glad of it because Buddy knew animals much better than Joe did. I did have to admit, though, Joe couldn't have chosen a better horse for me than Kit.

Lenore Sylvain Dexter

On Christmas morning, Buddy opened the kitchen door and yelled, "Miss Bernice! Come on outside here right now!" We were having a later breakfast than usual because it was the holiday. I had managed to hide away a little money, so I was able to buy Bernice a couple of modest presents from Sam's store for her to open that morning. It didn't take much to please Bernice. She was such a sweet little girl. The candy and fruit would have pleased her plenty, but I had Cora ask Sam to order a baby doll for Bernice, and she was so excited when she saw it. She wouldn't let go of that doll once she got her hands on it. She named her Kitty.

But at that moment, hearing Buddy, she went from looking like a happy-faced kid to a terrified one. Because she was so used to Joe's hollering, she just assumed she was in trouble with Buddy. "Go on now, Bernice," I said. "Go see what Buddy wants." Very slowly and timidly, Bernice slipped her coat and boots on and walked out. I shrugged my own coat on and was right behind her. I couldn't wait to see the look on her face.

Buddy had the pony around the corner of the house, so she didn't see it right off. She called, "Buddy?"

He answered, "Over here." She followed his voice.

I wasn't disappointed when I saw her reaction. Her eyes got big, her mouth opened wide, and she exclaimed, "Who's that!?"

Buddy grinned and answered, "Well, the people who had her called her Bonny, but since she's yours now, you can name her anything you want to."

"She's mine?"

"Yep! All yours. It's a gift from your Mama and Papa."

"From Papa?"

Sugarhouse Trials

I answered that question. "Yes, Bernice. Wasn't that nice of Papa?"

"Are you *sure* Papa will let me keep her?"

By this time, Joe was out there with us, and he said sternly, "As long as you stay a good girl and do your chores and take care of her, I'll let you keep her, but if I see you're not doing what you're supposed to, she's going back. Understand?"

"Yes, Papa. Thank you, Papa. I'll take real good care of Bonny just like Mama cares for Kit." Joe just grunted and turned away.

That was a good day in the Fletcher household. I wanted to believe that maybe there was hope for Joe yet.

CHAPTER THIRTY

The following spring, I had a suspicion that I might be pregnant. Things just weren't the same with my body. I noticed my middle was getting a bit thicker and I had some unusual cravings for foods I normally wouldn't eat, not to mention my monthlies not coming around. But I kept that to myself. For some reason, Joe always aimed for my head when he hit me, so I wasn't too concerned about this new little one inside of me. I still thought it might not be a good idea to let Joe know. I knew he would accuse me of being unfaithful.

But it wasn't too long after that everything changed. I was in the barn tending to Kit, combing him down with the curry comb. It always soothed me to be with Kit. I knew unconditional love with him, and our time together was peaceful and uncomplicated. I could only ride him if Joe was away on an errand or passed out drunk. He hated for me to go anywhere alone. I knew it was because he thought I was meeting Leo or Otis somewhere. While

I was enjoying that peace and connection with my horse, Joe came storming into the barn. Kit reared up and neighed like he knew Joe was on the rampage. "Whoa, boy," I said soothingly. I turned to face Joe. He was red in the face, looking like he could murder someone. I was afraid that someone might be me.

"I just talked to Otis, you no-good whore of a wife!" He kicked me in the stomach. I bent over in pain, silently saying a prayer for my baby. Luckily, he didn't kick too hard, because I'd seen him raise his leg and managed to step back a hair, but still...I felt very protective of this unborn baby. I gasped.

"He tole me the two of y'all were leaving and goin' to New Hampshire, and he'd kill me if I got in the way!"

My heart sank. I knew Otis was a little "off," and I'd been afraid he'd end up saying something stupid.

"Oh, for cryin' out loud, Joe! Be serious. You know I wouldn't be that foolish. Otis got some bee in his bonnet and doesn't know what the hell he's talking about. You're not gonna believe him, are you? I keep telling you there's nothing going on between me and Otis. He's just not right in his mind. Buddy even told you that!"

Joe, of course, had been drinking, so he looked confused. "I'm firing him, Anna. It ain't been any good since he came here. You were wrong ta hire him. It's your fault!" He huffed his way out of the barn. I slumped down on the ground, feeling defeated. Kit put his head down and nudged me. I felt so hopeless, helpless, and defenseless. I knew that if he did fire Otis, we'd either have to hire someone else or kiss our working farm good-bye.

Little did I know that Otis was close by when he saw Joe stomp into the barn. He had followed him in and hidden behind the

Sugarhouse Trials

creamery door while Joe was on his tirade. He heard and saw everything. Coming out of his hiding place, he exclaimed, "Anna, this has got to stop, ya know?! What do you want to do?"

I jumped at the sound of his voice. "You scared me, Otis! Don't be jumping out at me like that! And WHY would you tell him I was going away with you? You're just making it worse! You know you're going to get fired, right? I'm pregnant with *his* child!"

Otis looked at me, horrified, and said, "Wish it were *my* baby you was havin', ya know…then I'd have a definite reason ta get rid of him."

Another one of Otis's foolish remarks. I smiled, shook my head sadly, and said, feeling utterly defeated, "Go on home to Wilma, Otis. Go make a baby with *her!*" I looked back down and wept.

Otis stood there, staring at me for a couple of minutes. When I looked up, I saw he was still there with a strange look on his face. I could see that he was contemplating something in that simple brain of his.

"I know what ta do, Anna, and I'm gonna fix it, ya know."

CHAPTER THIRTY-ONE

All the next week, I did my best to stay away from Joe. He did end up firing Otis the very next day. Buddy and I mulled it over, trying to decide what would be the best thing to do. Because Joe's reputation was so marred, I doubted anyone would even want to come work for us. Buddy said, "You know, Anna, this whole problem is Joe's doing. Why don't we just sit back and let *him* decide? You know whatever we decide, he'll just yell and complain. I say, let's just do what we can do and when certain duties don't get done, he'll either have to shape up or try to hire someone else."

"You're right, Buddy." I sighed dejectedly. "But I also know that I'll get blamed in any event."

Surprisingly, Buddy wrapped his big, burly arms around me and gave me a hug. "How 'bout we just take it one day at a time and see what happens?" Buddy never gave hugs, so this gesture just made me cry harder.

Because of what Otis told Joe, I noticed Joe keeping a much closer eye on me. It seemed that whenever I turned around, I saw him looking at me with distrust. I didn't like it one bit. I remembered there was a time when I couldn't get enough of looking at him, but now I hated the sight of him. I liked it better when he'd just escape to his little sugarhouse hideaway and leave me alone.

It was a few weeks after Joe fired Otis that he sat at the kitchen table drinking his whiskey while I cooked supper. "Joe, go on now…I'm not going to run away with Otis. Please just leave me be. I hate you following me around!" I was making stew, stirring it so it wouldn't stick to the bottom of the pan.

"Too bad, little missy…you ain't trustworthy, and no way am I gonna let you make a laughingstock outta me by leaving with that hair-brained freak."

I couldn't help myself as I mumbled under my breath, "You don't need anybody but yourself to make people laugh at you."

He came out of his chair as quick as a jackrabbit and grabbed my arm. "What did y'all say to me!?!" he thundered. The next thing I knew, he picked up the pot of stew and threw it down at my feet. The heavy pot hit my left foot, and not only did it hurt from the weight of the pot, but the boiling liquid went through my slipper and stocking, and the burn was agonizing. I screamed. Cora and Bernice came running. When Joe saw them, he growled, "Bitch!" and left, slamming the kitchen door.

Both Cora and Bernice came up to me, and Bernice started crying, "Mama, are you okay?"

And Cora asked, "What happened? Come, Anna, sit down."

"My foot, Cora," I cried. She knelt down on the floor in front of me as I sat, and she took off my slipper. Not only was my foot quickly becoming twice the size of the other one, there were already blisters popping up.

"My God, Anna, was this an accident?"

I looked at her through watery eyes and gave her a little shake of my head.

"That man is truly the devil!" she exclaimed. "How could he do something like this? We need to get you to Doc Shepherd."

"No, Cora," I managed. "We mustn't tell anyone about this. You can put some of that salve we have on it and the swelling will go down eventually. I don't think my foot's broken."

"I'll do it, Anna, but if your foot isn't any better in a couple of days, I'll get Buddy to pick you up and carry you to Doc's, ya hear?"

"Okay, Cora. Bernice, run up to my room and fetch the salve I need. It's in the top drawer of my chest, okay? You'll do that for Mama?"

Bernice was holding on to me for dear life. "Okay, Mama, I will," she said sadly, "but I hate Papa Joe. I wish he'd just go away." I couldn't help but agree with her.

That evening, Joe went to the sugarhouse. After our little episode, he seemed not to hover as much. It was sugaring season. He liked it and was able to handle the tedious boiling process of making syrup since it took several hours and didn't require much physical labor; but for Joe, it was a solitary job and something he could master with only one good hand. It was the only thing he was willing to help with.

I was relieved he would be gone for a while. Maybe he'd just pass out and spend the night there, I hoped. Peaceful nights were few and far between for me now.

I excused myself early that night and headed off to bed. My foot still hurt badly, and it helped when I elevated it. Cora said she'd help Bernice get ready for bed and she'd see me in the morning. We said our good-nights, and I very carefully hobbled up the stairs. I felt on edge as I prepared for bed. I thought about Otis, remembering what he'd said. "I'm gonna fix it."

A few weeks later, early on the morning of April 29, I went downstairs to start breakfast. It was a Saturday. Joe wasn't in the parlor like he usually was, spread out on the couch. I made hotcakes and bacon and was warming the maple syrup when Bernice and Cora wandered into the kitchen. "Oh boy, Mama, I smell pannycakes!" Bernice said excitedly.

"Why, yes, you do, sweet girl…go wash up now." I looked over at Cora, who was smiling after Bernice as she skipped away to the sink.

"Joe didn't make it into the house last night, Cora. I have an uneasy feeling."

"Aww…he probably was too drunk to walk so he stayed where he was. He knew Buddy wasn't going to be around to feed the animals this morning. I heard him tell Buddy he'd take care of it. He probably woke up from wherever he was and went to the barn. Bernice and I'll take a walk after we eat to see if he's in there," Cora offered.

What Cora said made sense to me. Buddy had made mention yesterday that he was going to Papa's early in the morning to borrow his oxen and plow, so he wouldn't be able to feed the livestock. I was surprised when Joe said he would handle it.

CHAPTER THIRTY-TWO

"He ain't in the barn, Anna," Cora came back and reported as I was cleaning up the breakfast dishes. "Looks like none of the livestock's been taken care of, either. So much for Joe keeping his word."

The uneasy feeling stirred in my gut again. "Maybe we should go check the sugarhouse. Maybe he got so drunk he fell and he's hurt. Give me a minute and we'll all go check it out together."

"You think Papa Joe is hurt, Mama?" Concern was written all over her sweet little face. She'd seen too much hurt already in her short life.

"I don't think so, Bernice, but we'll go check, and if he is, we'll help him, okay?"

"Okay," she said sadly.

Because of my foot, the three of us walked slowly. The animals were hungry and were letting us know. When we got to the sugarhouse, I felt that jittery feeling again and asked Cora if she would mind going in first.

What she found would surely be etched into her brain forever. I noted Cora's eyes as she turned around to face Bernice and me. She was shaking her head, and her eyes were wide and scared. I told Bernice to go fetch apples for Kit and Bonny to hold them over until we fed them. I told her they were really hungry and they were waiting on her. "Okay, Mama!" With glee, she ran toward the barn.

With Bernice out of earshot, Cora exclaimed, "Anna, I think Joe's dead! He's in there, all right. He's lying facedown on the floor and his clothes are all bloody." Cora looked like she was going to cry.

"Go stay with Bernice, Cora. I'm gonna go check it out." Cora nodded and left.

Slowly, I opened the door and immediately smelled the metallic scent of blood, like when we butchered our hogs. Just like Cora said, Joe was lying there facedown, and there was blood everywhere. I ran out and vomited my breakfast. Shakily, I went back in; I could see the rifle underneath his body. I called to him three times, but he didn't respond. Deep down, I knew he was dead, but my mind had a hard time accepting it. *What should I do?* I decided to go get Papa. I limped as fast as I could, but there was still snow on the ground. It was slippery and I was thinking of the baby…I didn't want to fall. I was totally out of breath when I finally went crashing through my parents' kitchen door.

They were sitting at the table drinking coffee. "Anna? Are you okay? What is it? Why are you limping?" Mama spoke first. They

Sugarhouse Trials

both looked shocked to see me, especially since I was practically hysterical.

I collapsed onto a chair. Tears streamed down my face. "Oh my God! I think Joe's dead!"

"What? What are you talking about, Anna?" Papa exclaimed.

"He's in the sugarhouse, but he's all bloody and he's not moving."

Papa got out of his chair quicker than I would ever imagine he could. Mama just stood there in shock with her mouth open, staring at me.

"Come on, Anna, show me," said Papa. Papa hitched his horse to the buggy and it didn't take long to get to our sugarhouse. I felt numb, wondering if I was dreaming this nightmare. I didn't want to see Joe like that again, so I told Papa I would wait in the buggy. He nodded and got out, walking slowly to the door, and went inside. A minute later, he came back out and reached out to steady himself against the side of the building. I got out of the buggy and ran to him, afraid he might fall.

"Joe's gone, Anna girl."

"What should we do, Papa?" I trembled.

"I think you should go to Leo's and send him to fetch Dr. Shepherd, just to be sure."

"Okay, Papa. I'll do that. Maybe you should go on home to be with Mama."

Jumping onto Kit, I rode as fast as I could to Leo's house. I banged on the door, and his father saw me through the wired window screen. "Mr. Decker...where's Leo? I need him!" I yelled.

"I think he's out in the sugarhouse, Anna. Is everything okay? What's the matter?"

"Sorry, Mr. Decker…I gotta go get Leo."

I'm sure he must have watched me as I limped toward Leo, puzzled at my behavior. I did find Leo pretty quick, and after filling him in on the details, he took control and said, "Anna, go back home to be with Bernice. I'll take care of this; don't worry." Because I didn't know what else to do, I did what he asked and was thankful.

CHAPTER THIRTY-THREE

When I got home, I saw that Cora was trying to hold it together for Bernice. She was doing a pretty good job of it because Bernice was sitting at the table munching on a piece of cornbread, drinking milk, and babbling away. "Cora and I fed all the animals, Mama. She said I helped a lot 'cause I did everything right."

"I'm sure you did, baby. Thanks, Cora, for doing that. I don't know what I'd do without you. To tell you the truth, I forgot all about those poor animals."

When Cora looked at me, without saying a word, I knew my shocked expression mirrored hers. This was a nightmare. Was Joe really dead? Cora whispered, "Would he finally give up and shoot himself?" I could tell Cora wanted to talk about it. My head was about to explode.

I nodded at Cora and said, "Bernice, honey, do Mama a favor and go on down to the root cellar. I'm thinking about making a berry pie and I need some of those berries you helped me can. Think you can find them?"

"Oh, yes, Mama! I'll find them. I love berry pie! Can I help you make it?"

"Of course, Bernice...we'll make two and take one on over to Leo tomorrow."

"Goody! I'll be right back!" She happily complied. I knew it would take her a little bit to find them. *I* wasn't even sure where they were.

"Oh, Cora!" We fell into each other's arms and sobbed.

"This can't be really happening, Anna, can it?" she asked hesitantly.

"I know how you feel, Cora...but Papa confirmed he's dead. Leo went to get Doc Shepherd. He should be able to tell what happened to Joe. I feel so guilty because for the past few months I was wishing him dead. Now he is, and I don't know what to think! I'm so grateful you're here with me and Bernice."

A while later, as we were talking, I heard a commotion in the yard. Word travels fast in small towns, and I saw some of our neighbors heading toward Joe in the shack. Doc Shepherd and Leo were leading the crowd. Cora and I went outside to join them. Doc Shepherd went into the shack alone and came back out a few minutes later, shaking his head. Right about that time, two men rode in. I recognized the man with a thick handlebar mustache as the town health officer, George Williams, and the other was Howard Galt, who was our local sheriff. They were walking purposefully toward the sugarhouse and stopped to have a word with the Doc. I'm sure Sheriff Galt, who handled everything from barking dogs to corralling the town drunks, couldn't remember the last time there was a suspicious death in West Langford. That just didn't happen in this quiet little town. Cora and I walked outside and were almost at the scene when I saw Mama, Ella, Papa, and the boys standing to the side. Everyone seemed to be staring at me. When Mama saw me, she ran right up to me and held me. "I'm so sorry, baby. What can I do to help?"

For some reason, I still had a little bit of my wits about me. The mother in *me* said, "Thanks, Mama; would you please go down to the root cellar? Bernice is there getting berries. You need to distract her. I told her we were going to make berry pies...could you do that with her?"

"Of course, Anna. Whatever you need." I felt like a little girl again as Mama held me, and I let myself be comforted by this amazing woman who helped me through all the hurts in my life. I cried...not only for my dead husband, but also for this broken woman I had become.

"It's okay, Anna...everything's going to be okay. Papa and I love you. We'll help you through this." And off she went. I felt much better knowing Bernice would be distracted for a while. After composing myself, I turned, surveying the scene. It felt surreal to me, as if I weren't really there, but rather watching from another dimension.

The whole crowd was standing around the sugarhouse like they were waiting for something. I noticed that Doug and Lonny were standing with Otis. Otis was saying something to Doug. After a while, Dr. Shepherd, the sheriff, and Mr. Williams came back out. They had examined Joe's body and said Joe had been dead for some hours. Because of the way Joe was positioned, they were ruling out suicide...said the bullet smashed through his temple, broke his jaw, blew his brains out, and exited through the other side of his head. The death was instantaneous. Surely this was murder! But an autopsy had to be performed to be sure. At these words, everything went black.

When I awoke, I was on Joe's parlor couch with a cool cloth on my head. I could smell the sweet smell of Mama's pies in the air, and I forgot where I was and what was going on. Mama and Ella were staring at me. "Smells so good in here." I sat up and realized I was in my own parlor. Then it hit me...*Joe.*

"How's Joe?" I asked in a daze.

"Anna," Ella announced, "he's *dead.* Doc Shepherd said he was murdered. What do *you* know about that?"

Mama said, "Hush, Ella...leave Anna alone. She's in shock."

"He's really dead, then?" I asked.

"Umm...Anna, you and Cora are the ones who found him. Don't you remember?" Mama asked soothingly.

I went back in my mind. "I thought I mighta dreamed it, Mama. He's really gone?"

"Yes, Anna. I'm afraid so."

"Where's Bernice...does she know?"

"She's with Papa and Doug right now. She'll be fine. Papa will know what to say."

"What happened? Did they say Joe committed suicide?"

Ella was ruthless. "No, definitely not suicide. They're saying he was murdered. Do *you* have any idea who would have killed him, Anna??"

I couldn't seem to form thoughts in my head. "No!! I don't know!!" I started to cry.

PART FOUR

CHAPTER THIRTY-FOUR

Mama insisted on staying that first night with me. She said Cora needed a break and should go home. Buddy heard the news once he returned the oxen and plow to Papa. He had borrowed it to help ol' man Jenkins make a way to the main road. Jenkins had to be in his eighties, and when people hadn't heard from him in a while, his neighbor, Jack Parson, trudged through the snow to check on him. He was okay but getting low on supplies. Jack asked Buddy for help, and Buddy was willing.

As soon as Buddy heard about Joe, he was at our farm, making sure everything was taken care of. "I'll be here for you, Anna; don't you even have a worry about the farm...I'll take care of running it and if there's anything else I can do for ya, just please let me know."

"Thank you, Buddy. You and Cora are my rocks. I'm so blessed to have you in my life." Even though I knew he would feel uncomfortable, I hugged him and didn't feel awkward when he didn't hug back.

He said, "Ya know, Anna, when I first met Joe, I was very impressed with his determination and persistence about being a farmer. He knew pretty much nothing about farming. But he seemed to love it and caught on pretty quick. I saw him as a good student, a good boss, a good man, but most of all, a good husband and father. When he had that accident, it sure made him a *changed* man. I'm sorry for your loss, Anna. You've been without your husband for many a year now, not just a day. I'm happy and privileged to be able to help you through your sorrow."

I hugged him again, tighter this time, and said with teary eyes and a whisper, "Thank you for those words, Buddy. You're right. Joe *was* a good man and I'll always treasure *those* memories because that's who he really was. You're like a second father to me, and I will always treasure you in my heart." I think I really embarrassed him at that point, because he gave my shoulders a squeeze, turned around, and headed for the barn without a word.

CHAPTER THIRTY-FIVE

The authorities were like flies on manure in our sugarhouse for days. They didn't bother me. Not one of them came to the door asking for a drink or even to use our water closet. I later learned, through Papa, that they had determined the rifle used to kill Joe belonged to Otis. Leo had checked to see where Joe's rifle was at some point. He told me not to touch it or even go near it. It was in the far corner of the barn where we kept the feed. I wished Joe had taken his own life so we wouldn't have to all go through the horror of murder. Every time I heard the word *murder*, my heart raced.

On the afternoon of Joe's death, his body was sent to the Woods River schoolhouse for an autopsy. They asked Dr. Adam Stone to perform it and he, in turn, asked our own Dr. Shepherd to assist. They both concurred that it was indeed murder and not suicide. Leo told me he heard that they also determined that the body was moved to look like a suicide. Immediately, an inquest was scheduled, and family and friends were now being questioned.

I knew Otis had a thing for me and that he had threatened to kill Joe many times. Otis wasn't right in his head. He was certainly the person who was the likeliest suspect.

Of course, being Joe's wife, I was one of the first to be questioned. Mr. Williams came to my house the day after the autopsy was performed. He asked to speak with me, Cora, and Buddy. What did we remember the night he was murdered; did we see or hear anything that night? Where were we precisely; did we have contact with him, and on and on and on. It was emotionally exhausting. Then he said he wanted to talk to us separately. Buddy answered a few questions and told him he had to get back to work. He hadn't even been there that night or the morning of the incident, but he said he'd be available for more questioning in the evening if need be. Mr. Williams excused him and said he'd be in touch.

Cora went first while I took a walk to the barn to brush Kit. I was a jumble of nerves, but it did comfort me to tend to my beloved horse. Bernice was at my parents' and was to spend the night there. I thought that maybe after my questioning, I would go there, too. The thought of curling up in my old bed in my childhood bedroom sounded like heaven to me. I wasn't comfortable in my own home anymore…especially at night.

Mr. Williams found me in the barn and told me it was my turn. He had sent Cora home and told me he only needed a few minutes of my time. I followed him back into the kitchen and sat down heavily on the chair facing him. Again, with all the same kind of

Sugarhouse Trials

questions: Did you have marital problems? Were you involved with another man? Was there anyone who wanted Joe dead? I was as honest as I could be. Yes, we had problems. I explained about Joe's accident and how he had changed, started drinking, and had become abusive. No, I was never involved with another man. Otis was the only one who ever threatened Joe's life. (I did remember Leo saying he was going to kill Joe that first time Joe hit me, but I knew it was just a figure of speech and Leo didn't mean it, so I didn't mention that.) After about a half hour, Mr. Williams got up and said he'd be in touch. "Don't be going anywhere, now."

Ha, I thought. *Where would I go and why would I leave?*

Now I had to send a telegram to Joe's family with the news. When Joe had his accident, his father sent Joe's oldest brother, Ethan, to check out the situation. Joe didn't appreciate it and was surly. He wouldn't even talk to his brother except to say, "Go on back home, Ethan…we don't need your sympathy." I apologized to Ethan and thanked him for coming. He slipped me some money and told me it was from his Pa, and that if I needed anything, to just let them know. Joe would have been livid if he knew I took the money. He'd say we weren't a charity case, but I knew eventually we were gonna need that money, so I thanked Ethan and hid it away. Now, I wondered how they were going to take the news of murder as the cause of his death. Would they blame me? I dreaded coming face-to-face with the people I had come to love and who were Joe's family long before I was.

Leo was right there to support me while I was going through this hell. He told me that Mr. Williams had visited him also and asked him a lot of the same questions…specifically, if he and I were intimate. Leo again stood by me and said, "No, sir."

Apparently, somebody had mentioned that Leo and I were close. He was my best friend and was a comfort to me. I felt that I could confide in him. Buddy assured me that he and Cora would also stand by my side and help as much as they could. No one mentioned or talked about Otis, and I wondered if they all told Mr. Williams the same as I did—that Otis could have been the *only* one who pulled the trigger.

CHAPTER THIRTY-SIX

I sent a telegram to Joe's father informing him about the details of Joe's death. We had Joe's funeral the day after Mr. Fletcher and Ethan arrived from Louisiana. Mr. Fletcher and Ethan took a room at Mabel's boarding house, the same place Joe had stayed when he first came to West Langford. They both came to my door the evening before the service. My heart pounded when I saw Joe's father, not knowing how he would react to me. I got one of his bear hugs, and that one hug told me everything between us was okay.

Mr. Fletcher told me that Joe's mother was too ill to make the trip. Joe's death was hard on her, and she had taken to her bed. That made me feel so very sad. Both Mr. Fletcher and Ethan were nothing but kind to Bernice and me, and they even offered to take us back to their home in Louisiana to live. I thanked them mightily but told them that our home was here in West Langford, and we'd make do somehow with the help of family and friends.

Lenore Sylvain Dexter

The next morning, the day of Joe's funeral, was cloudy, glum, and depressing. It was a very "gray day." As I stood there looking at his plain pine casket, I couldn't help but be reminded of my old Joe. The Joe with the dark, penetrating eyes, who adored me and Bernice; the thoughtful Joe, who had bought me Kit; the gentle Joe, who was a tender lover. The Joe who didn't know anything about farming when he arrived in West Langford but worked long and hard at becoming the best farmer he could be.

I wept silently through the whole service. Brave little Bernice stood by my side. Because she really only remembered the mean Papa Joe, his death didn't affect her like it did me. Mr. Fletcher stood on the other side of me, with his hand gently on my back to give me support. As they lowered Joe's casket into the ground, a light rain began to fall. Mrs. Rowland, the church choir leader, started singing "Amazing Grace," and it seemed like the saddest song I had ever heard. I wept and couldn't remember ever feeling so sad. Cora had stayed home and with the help of a few neighbor ladies was setting up a spread so the people who attended the funeral could go back to our farm and have refreshments. Leo offered to escort me back to the house, but I told him it wouldn't look good. "I'll go back with Mama and Papa, but thanks for being here for me, Leo. It does help my heart a bit."

Mr. Fletcher and Ethan spent the night but had to get back to Louisiana the next day to tend to their business. When they were about to leave, Mr. Fletcher handed me a roll of dollar bills. He hugged me. "Just want you to know, Anna, that if you and Bernice ever need help, our family will be there for y'all."

Sugarhouse Trials

"Thank you kindly, Mr. Fletcher. I sure do wish things coulda been different. Joe and I used to be so happy." I broke down and cried again. He gave me one of his fierce hugs, and with tears in his own eyes, he nodded and walked away from me with Ethan.

CHAPTER THIRTY-SEVEN

I heard the next day that Otis was arrested for suspicion of Joe's murder as he was preparing to go to Joe's funeral. I had wondered why I hadn't seen him or Wilma at the service. That same day, he was put in Orange County's jail, which was in Chelsea, about twenty miles from West Langford. I still thought Otis was the only one who could be blamed for this horrible crime. Part of me wanted to help him, but I wasn't sure how to do that. I did go by to see Wilma one day to comfort her, but she wouldn't let me in. She told me I wasn't her friend. "Go away and never come back! I hate you, Anna Fletcher! You stole my husband!" That shook me up pretty badly, but I respected her wishes and slowly walked back home.

CHAPTER THIRTY-EIGHT

Otis hired a lawyer by the name of Roy Barber. I had heard that his trial was going to be held in July. One day in early June, I was weeding in our garden when Leo galloped into my yard on his horse.

By now I was starting to show, and most of the people I knew were aware I was with child. When Leo first found out, he asked me some personal questions. If it had been anybody else but Leo, I would have said, "Mind your own business!"

When I saw him coming, I got up and stretched my back, thinking it was a friendly visit. With Joe gone, Leo was a regular visitor to our home. When he got off his horse, he came slowly up to me. "Hey, Anna…come in the house with me."

"Why…what's going on, Leo?"

"First come with me. I need to tell you something and I want you to sit down."

I had a bad feeling and got a sudden chill, even though the weather was quite warm. Once we were inside, he sat me down. He took a chair, turned it around, and sat across from me, straddling it. He took both my hands in his. "I just heard from Hal Jenkins that Otis is telling people that it was your idea to murder Joe. Said you were pregnant with his child and the two of you were planning on killing Joe, taking Bernice, and running away!"

"What?? That's a **lie**, Leo!! You know that, right?" I was sure my eyes were as round as the saucers sitting in my cupboard.

"Of course I do, Anna. Do you really need to ask me that?" I could see the hurt in his eyes.

"No; of course not, Leo. It's just that…that…" Stupid tears, then sobs racked my body. Everything came crashing down on me. I couldn't help but feel guilty.

"What'll I *do*, Leo?" I needed his calm manner.

He squeezed both my hands. "Well, I'm thinking first thing is we gotta get you a lawyer! Let me ask around. I'll talk to your Pa. There's gotta be a good defense lawyer that we can hire."

"Okay, Leo…I got the money Joe's father gave me…we can use that."

"I got money, too, Anna. You know I'll help you any way I can."

We got up, and I fell into Leo's arms. He tilted my head and kissed me, a long, deep kiss. "You know I love you, Anna. I think I've loved you forever."

Leo and Papa put their heads together and found me a lawyer by the name of Bradley Holcomb. Leo told me Otis's confession claimed that he met me at my house after Joe went to the sugarhouse that night. "It was Anna," he said, "who decided it would be a good night to get rid of Joe." He said I told him to go get his rifle and come back around 11:00. Apparently, I said that Joe would probably be drunk as a skunk by that time and we'd have an easier time of it. There was a knothole on the side of the shack. A rifle would fit in there for a perfect shot. Otis said he agreed, and we both trekked down to the sugarhouse a little after 11 p.m. Otis told his lawyer that once we got there, he decided he didn't want to go through with it, so I grabbed his rifle and shot Joe myself.

It was a convincing story, and knowing how Joe was, a lot of people would probably believe it. I was devastated. I'd known Otis was a liar because of all the times he'd lied to Joe and Buddy, but I never thought he'd put the blame on me!

CHAPTER THIRTY-NINE

It was a couple days later when the authorities came to my door to arrest me. There were two of them...very serious-looking. One of the men, who introduced himself as Jeffrey Connor, told us they were from Orange County Jail. I knew that was where Otis was being held. He then introduced his partner as Lawrence Boudreaux. I was happy that Leo happened to be with me at the time, even though it was early morning. I needed someone strong to lean on. Cora was upstairs changing the bedsheets, and Bernice, thank goodness, was in the barn with the horses. I asked the bailiff for a minute so I could call Cora down. She looked shocked when I told her what was happening. "I'm gonna need you to look after Bernice for a bit, Cora. Mama and Papa will no doubt help with her, but I'm not quite sure how long I'll be gone."

Cora, with tears in her eyes, said, "You bet, Anna. Between Buddy, Leo, and me, we'll make sure to run everything around here. You take care, ya hear?" She wrapped me in her arms and hugged hard.

The bailiff said, "Okay, Mrs. Fletcher, time to go."

Leo told me he would follow along so he could be with me while they did the processing. I looked at him with grateful eyes and said, "Oh, thank you, Leo…I do need you right now." Under different circumstances, I'm sure those words would have thrilled Leo, but unfortunately, that wasn't the case now.

With tears in my eyes, I said, "Cora, I just can't bring myself to say good-bye to Bernice right now. I'm afraid I'd only make it worse for her if she saw the mess I am."

Sadly, and with her own tearful eyes, she said, "I'll handle it; don't worry. I'll just tell her you had to go away for a little while for family business or something. Maybe I'll take her and Bonny to my house for a couple of days as a distraction. I think she'd like that. You know we love to spoil her."

I hugged her, "Can't thank you enough, Cora. You're like a sister to me," I managed with a watery smile.

CHAPTER FORTY

The ride to the jail was and still is a blur to me. I remember getting into a vehicle, and the next thing I remember, we were in a cold, dreary room with people asking me all kinds of questions. It was quite overwhelming, and I'd never been so afraid in my life. Leo got permission to come in with me and stood behind the hard, straight-backed chair I was sitting in with his hands on my shoulders. His presence was a comfort, and I was so grateful for it. There was a large gray desk in front of me, where a man sat rigidly. Two other chairs were in the corner, where two other men sat.

The person asking most of the questions was a man by the name of Mr. Tinker. He was tall and wiry with a big beak nose and small eyes. It was hard for me not to stare at his nose. It seemed way too big for his face, and I had to fight to concentrate on his eyes. If he were a bird, he would have been an eagle by the looks of him.

Lenore Sylvain Dexter

"Where were you the night your husband was murdered, Mrs. Fletcher?"

"I was home with my husband, daughter, and housekeeper, Cora," I answered.

"What do you remember about the night before your husband was found?"

I proceeded to tell him all the facts…how Joe went to the sugaring house to boil down his last sap run. Not knowing if Mr. Tinker knew about Joe's drinking habits, I told him that Joe always had a stash of whiskey and cider in there, and sometimes he would pass out and stay the night.

"And you don't recall any gunshot sounds? Anything unusual?"

"No, sir. By the time all my chores are done and I'm upstairs in my bed, I'm out like a light. Besides, I had hurt my foot a couple of days before and needed to rest it. I took an old pain pill from when Joe had his accident, and that put me out cold. I doubt Cora heard anything, either; otherwise, she would have mentioned it to me in the morning. She was in the bedroom next to mine."

"What happened when you got up in the morning?"

Again, I explained it all. How we noticed he wasn't on the sofa like he usually was and how he had told our farmhand he would feed the animals for him because Buddy couldn't do it that morning—but that the animals hadn't been tended to. Cora and Bernice checked the barn, but he wasn't there. I told him how next we went to the sugarhouse and how I had a bad feeling, so I asked Cora to go in first.

"You had a bad feeling? Why did you have a bad feeling?"

"Because years ago, when Joe had his accident, he became a very different man. He hated himself and everyone else. I often wondered at times if he would take his own life. It was something I thought he might do someday."

"But you know, don't you, that he didn't take his life. He was murdered in cold blood." He said it so accusingly that I flinched. I took a deep breath as Leo squeezed my shoulders. I knew it was his silent way of saying, *Be strong, now.*

I found some strength in that and said, "Mr. Tinker, my husband was not a nice man at the end, but I would never take another person's life...especially the father of my two children. I'm expecting his second child by the end of the year."

"Well, Mrs. Fletcher, I'm afraid we're still going to have to hold you here until we get this thing all sorted out. I am assuming you have a lawyer?"

"Yes, sir, I do. His name is Bradley Holcomb. He's from Barre."

"That's good, Mrs. Fletcher. I know the man, and if all that you're saying is true, I guess he'd be the one to save you."

I turned around and looked at Leo. Like me, he had tears in his eyes as he said, "We're gonna make this right, Anna; I promise." I stood and wrapped my arms around him, trying to stifle my sobs.

"Thanks, Leo. Please go check on Bernice for me."

"I will, Anna, ya know I will. I'll take good care of her. I'll go let your folks know what's happening, too."

CHAPTER FORTY-ONE

Right about that time, a very rough-looking man came out to take me away. What kind of nightmare was *this??* One last glance at Leo, and I went with the guard. The two of us walked down a long, smelly corridor. He took a key out and unlocked a big steel door. It went from silence to unbearable noise. I heard yelling and screaming and crying and cussing. I was so shaken I felt like I could collapse. What was I, Anna Roberts Fletcher, doing in a place like this? I wanted to yell and cry and cuss myself.

I was led to a small cell with two cots. One looked as if it had been used, so I assumed the other was for me. There was a blanket folded up on the bottom of the bed along with a yellow-stained pillow on top of it. I cringed. I could definitely sleep without a pillow, I thought. There was a chamber pot in the corner, and I wondered who the lucky worker was who had the lovely job of emptying it. Maybe it would be *me*, I thought frantically.

I sat on my cot as the guard locked me in my cell. This was just too much. I felt like an animal in a cage. How would I ever survive this nightmare? I didn't often pray. We weren't brought up to be church folk, even though Mama and Papa were good Christian people. However, I found the words in my heart to ask God to help me know what to do and to help me cope for Bernice and the baby's sake. By this time, I was guessing I was about four months pregnant. A horrible thought entered my mind…would this baby be born here in jail? I immediately banished the thought. There was no way I would still be here come November, would I?

My cellmate was a woman named Thelma. She looked to be a few years older than me. Reluctantly, she told me she'd been in here for about a year because her husband ran away and left her with seven kids and a whole lot of debt she couldn't repay. It sure didn't seem fair to me. Why wasn't her no-good loser of a husband in jail? Women didn't have much say in those days. It made me sad and mad that Thelma was even there. I thought to myself, *This poor woman is taking the punishment of her husband and can't be with her children!* My situation was bad, probably worse than Thelma's, but I knew I would be proven innocent; I had a good lawyer, people to support me, and I had hope. Not so with Thelma.

Thelma was a lot like Wilma. She wasn't educated, and she seemed naïve and defeated. She was a tall woman, at least three inches taller than me. She had dark hair; thick, bushy eyebrows; and a very timid disposition. I tried to have a conversation with her a couple of times, but she wouldn't have it. She almost looked scared of me, like I might kill her in her sleep. I guess I couldn't blame her. I'm sure she'd heard the reason I was there and believed every word of it.

CHAPTER FORTY-TWO

My lawyer came to visit me the very next day. The guard came to get me, leading me into a small, windowless room with whitewashed walls. There was a small table in the middle with a hardback chair on either side. The guard sat me down in one of the chairs, and as he left to go out the only door, he said, "You behave yourself." I wondered why he would say that to me. I hadn't caused a lick of trouble since I arrived.

I sat there thinking of this when the door opened and in walked a man I believed to be my lawyer. I got up. "Mrs. Fletcher…I'm Attorney Holcomb. Have a seat." I noticed that his coat looked well-made, and I saw he had a gold pocket watch. He was a decent-looking man who appeared to be about fifty years old. He had wavy silver hair, a neatly trimmed beard, and kind eyes.

Before sitting, I extended my hand. "I'm very pleased to be meeting you, Mr. Holcomb. Thank you for helping me get out of this mess." His hands were soft, reminding me of the first time I touched Joe's hands.

"Mrs. Fletcher," he greeted me, "it *is* a mess and hopefully we will be able to get you out of it, but first I need to ask you some questions." He asked me pretty much all the same questions I was asked by Mr. Tinker, all the while taking notes on a piece of paper. Then, he got to talking about Otis.

"What do you actually know about Otis Hansen, Mrs. Fletcher?"

"Please, call me Anna."

"Okay, Anna; tell me about Otis."

"Well, when Joe wasn't able to do his share of chores around the farm after his accident, we needed help. Do you know about Joe's accident?"

"Yes, as a matter of fact, I do. Your father explained all of that to me."

"So you probably also know that we have a hired hand, Buddy, who is more like family. But our farm was too much for Buddy to take care of alone, so I hired Otis because we were desperate. Otis seemed a little backward but took direction from Buddy pretty well. He has a wife named Wilma, who, in my opinion, isn't any more intelligent than he is. They have no children that I know of. They live in the guesthouse at Hood's farm. After working with us awhile, I noticed Otis became way too interested in me."

"What do you mean, he was 'way too interested in you'?" Mr. Holcomb was frowning.

I squirmed in my seat a little. "Well, he used to say things like he'd leave Wilma for me and he'd like to kill Joe for hurting me.

Sugarhouse Trials

He once even told Joe that we had plans to run away together to New Hampshire!"

"Did you and Otis ever talk about doing that?"

"Oh my God!! No, no, and no! Not me! Otis talked about it, but never me!" I exclaimed. I was sure I sounded hysterical. "He made up that story when he found out Joe was hitting me. Otis knew how Joe was abusing me. He used to lie about things all the time. I told him to stop...that he was making everything worse. But to tell you the truth, I'm not sure what he had in his mind. He told me the last time we spoke that he was going to 'fix this problem.' I didn't know what he meant, until..." I was so worked up; I couldn't help myself. I put my head in my hands, and unattractive-sounding sobs came from I don't even know where. The good, compassionate lawyer leaned toward me and laid his hand on my shoulder. His empathy would normally have made me cry harder, but I thought, *Leo would tell me to "buck up" right about now*, so I held my breath for a moment. As I lifted my head with tears in my eyes, the lawyer sat up, too.

He squinted and looked into my eyes. "I have to ask you, Anna. Did you have anything—anything at all—to do with Joe's death?"

"No, Mr. Holcomb! I swear! I had nothing to do with it! I have a daughter and a baby on the way...I would never take the risk of losing them."

"Well, let me tell you what I learned about Otis Hansen." He then proceeded to tell me Otis's story of how he stole money from the family and all. I thought of Wilma and how Otis told her it was

221

all a lie...that his parents were the ones who lied. Otis was full of lies.

He looked at me and said sincerely, "I usually have good instincts about my clients, and I'd like to believe you, Anna. To believe that you are innocent. I'm going to try my best to clear you, but you are going to have to be strong and help me out here. Are you up for it?"

I sniffed back the tears and cleared my throat. "Yes, Mr. Holcomb...I am...I really think I am."

"Okay, Anna, we're probably going to be spending a lot of time together. So how 'bout you call me Brad, and we'll try to get you outta here as soon as possible to get you back with your little girl?"

CHAPTER FORTY-THREE

On the afternoon of July 18, Otis and I were led into the Orange County courtroom. The courthouse was jammed with inquisitive people on that hot July day. I tried to give Otis a tight smile as I walked past him, but it was impossible considering I wouldn't even be there if it weren't for him. He just stared back at me with no expression.

The court clerk began to read aloud the charges. "Anna Roberts Fletcher and Otis James Hansen, not fearing the wrath of God, willingly and knowingly planned and followed through with the execution of Joseph L. Fletcher on April 29, 1916."

The clerk now addressed me. "How do you plead?"

"Not guilty," I replied.

"How would you be tried?"

"By God and my country," I responded, as Brad told me this was the ritual answer.

Next, he directed his attention to Otis and asked the same questions. Otis answered the same as I did.

Both my lawyer and Otis's lawyer insisted on separate trials. The criminal justice officials agreed because they were hoping that a successful prosecution of Otis would hurry along my conviction. This upset me greatly when I heard of it, but Brad reassured me that I was innocent until proven guilty, so not to worry.

Our trials were truly the biggest homicide trials in Orange County. The Vermont Attorney General, Frank Jackson, was the prosecutor while Roy Barber and his legal team fought to defend Otis. The trial judge was Marvin Driscoll. I only had to stay for the judge to preside at our formal arraignment. Once I was arraigned, I was immediately brought back to my cell. Brad, of course, stayed to monitor what might help or hinder my case.

CHAPTER FORTY-FOUR

Such mixed feelings I had as I sat on my very uncomfortable cot going over what I had just witnessed in the courtroom. I couldn't believe all the people who had gathered for the trial. Was life that boring for them that they needed something like this for entertainment? I knew for a fact that all those people probably didn't know Joe or me and definitely not Otis. I felt pity for them.

The feelings I had for Otis were horror and confusion. It was still hard for me to believe he could do something so horrendous as to put all the blame on me while he was always telling me how much he loved me. The other feelings I had were fear and hope, and it was still hard to believe that this was really happening. It was scary to think that once Otis was done with his trial, it would be my turn. People would be judging me, and I could only hope that with my friends as witnesses and Brad defending me, I would be able to go home and live a normal life.

CHAPTER FORTY-FIVE

The next day, Brad came to fill me in on Otis's trial. The Attorney General's opening statement made it clear that the state would rely mostly on circumstantial evidence to convict Otis and me of premeditated murder. He told the jury that even though Otis was married to Wilma, shortly after I had hired him, the two of us began an intimate affair that lasted right up to the night of Joe's death. He said that everything escalated when I found out I was pregnant. Otis had told his wife about us and how he wanted to leave her and take me away to New Hampshire.

Then he went on to the night of the murder. The lawyer claimed that Otis went to my house a short time after Joe went to the sugarhouse. After being intimate, we then walked together to the sugarhouse. When we got there, one of us shot a bullet through Joseph Fletcher's head. Jackson said the murder was simply a process of elimination. Otis and I killed Joe so we could be together.

Lenore Sylvain Dexter

The defense answered Jackson's opening statement by asking the jury to keep an open mind about Otis's innocence before hearing all the evidence.

The state's first witness was Doc Shepherd, who was the first to examine the body. He stated how he had quickly concluded that Joe had been dead for several hours. Because of the suspicious position of the body and other things, the doc knew it couldn't have been a suicide. Since there were no powder burns on the body, he said that the shot had to have been fired from at least four feet away from the victim. Also, because of a trail of bloodstains on the floor, he believed the body was moved after death.

The state's second witness was Dr. Stone, who performed the autopsy. The jury was shown photographs and maps of the murder in our sugarhouse. Dr. Stone concurred that in no way could Joseph Fletcher's death have been a suicide. It made sense that someone did take the shot through the knothole in the wall.

At that, the prosecutors clarified the motive for the murder. They called Wilma next, and she testified that Otis had told her I was pregnant with his baby and we were going away together. Brad told me she could barely get the words out, she was so upset. She was forced to testify that the adultery caused difficulties in their marriage and she and Otis had decided to separate temporarily, but it only lasted a week because Otis had nowhere to go.

The state next called Darrell Sawyer. He was at the Halloween Festival that Otis and I attended. He attested that yes, I arrived with Otis, and yes, I spent the evening with him and Leo, dancing, drinking cider, and having a good time without my husband. After Otis had been drinking awhile, Darrell said that Otis and he were together at the bar when Otis confided in him that he and I were having an affair and that the two of us were going to New Hampshire together. Otis also told Darrell that I had offered him cash to kill Joe.

Then there was the testimony of the bailiff who arrested Otis. He claimed that Otis told him right away that he was innocent, he didn't pull the trigger, and that it was my idea to murder Joe, but Otis also said something contradictory, something about how he was as good as getting fried in the electric chair.

The state tried to get Cora to give evidence of our adultery when she was asked if she had seen us together on a regular basis. She admitted that she had seen Otis and me in the barn alone often, but it was because we were doing chores together. The lawyer asked to eliminate her last statement. The judge agreed, but the jury had heard it.

Leo was called as a witness. Unfortunately, I had told Otis that Leo was giving me a refresher course on rifle shooting. Otis told his lawyer about that. Leo admitted it but said it was for the purpose of self-defense if need be. The prosecutor didn't let him elaborate more than that.

Dr. James Shepherd was called back to the stand. He told how he was called to Otis's house around the beginning of April because Wilma had a stomach virus. Dr. Shepherd recounted some rather intimate confessions made to him by Otis. He told the doctor that he had been having "improper relations" with me for some time and that we were so smitten with each other that we were planning to run away together soon. He told the Doc that Joe

Fletcher was a mean bastard and he shouldn't deserve to live and put Anna through hell like he did.

One more incriminating witness was my brother Doug. He stated that on the day of the murder, he and Otis were standing side by side with the crowd at the sugarhouse. Once Otis heard Joe pronounced dead, he whispered to Doug, "Guess I'm the same as in the electric chair."

Lastly, they brought up the confession Otis had made in June. The court stenographer read aloud to the jury. Otis swore it was me who actually thought of the idea to get rid of Joe and then offered him money to do it. He swore again that I was the one who started the affair and that it was my idea to run away together. He then proceeded to say that I had contacted him on the day of the murder and told him to come to my house with his rifle at 11 p.m. He said when he arrived at my house, I already had my sweater on, was wearing a pair of Joe's boots, and had Joe's rifle in my hand. He swore he thought I was just taking the rifle to Joe in the sugarhouse. When we arrived at the sugarhouse, he claimed that he didn't think I was serious when I told him to go on and shoot Joe. He said he was shocked when I kept demanding that he take the shot. He said he refused repeatedly, so apparently, I grabbed his rifle away from him and shot Joe myself. Afterward, I made Otis move the body and place the rifle under it. He claimed when the deed was done, we then returned to my house to spend more time together before Otis went home for the night.

The state had consumed the better part of three court days and rested their case that Wednesday morning.

CHAPTER FORTY-SIX

The defense managed to squeeze in their witnesses that afternoon after a noon break.

Cora was first and told how even though Joe was brutal to me, she never heard anything from either Otis or me about murdering Joe. She did testify that I had confided in her about Otis's infatuation for me and how I thought it was silly and immature.

Buddy was next and told how Otis was simpleminded and said and did things that were not regular. He lied about everything and made up stories, so he never believed much of what Otis said. They asked Doc Shepherd and Darrell Sawyer why, when Otis confessed the affair with me, they didn't go to Joe and let him know what was going on. They admitted that Joe was a hard man to talk to and they really didn't want to get involved, but Doc Shepherd did agree with Buddy that he thought there was something "off" about Otis.

Leo was the last called to the stand. When asked what he thought of Otis, he admitted that Otis was a big help to Buddy at Anna's farm, but he always felt there was something a little slow-witted about the man and was sorry to say he never really trusted him.

The judge then proceeded to tell the jury that closing arguments would take place after a fifteen-minute break.

Once back in the courtroom, the prosecution's closing arguments stated that Joseph Fletcher's killers took their time to make his death look like a suicide. He said Otis Hansen and I had planned out this murder and carried it out according to Otis's confession. They determined that we both wanted Joseph L. Fletcher dead so we could be together!

Barber and his team's closing defense arguments were not what most expected. They actually conceded the truthfulness of some of Otis's confession. They admitted that adultery was probable, and because of that, Otis was most likely an accessory because of his infatuation with me. But no hard evidence, direct or circumstantial, in the confession or in any testimony, determined that Otis had actively taken part in the actual murder of Joseph Fletcher.

After both closing arguments, the judge instructed the twelve jurists to make their decision. He emphasized the presumption of innocence and the concept of reasonable doubt. He told them if they believed that Otis had an active part in the murder and knew about my plan to kill Joe, he was guilty of murder in the first degree. But if he only knew of the facts and did not actually have a part in Joe's murder, they might find him guilty of second-degree murder.

He then explained the additional verdicts of manslaughter or not guilty and proceeded to send them out.

It took the jury fifteen hours to decide their verdict. Brad was there when the jury made their announcement. He told me Otis looked very scared and pale when he was led into the courtroom. The jury found him guilty of second-degree murder, and he was led away to serve a mandatory life sentence in the Windsor prison.

Brad filed for a continuance due to my pregnancy. He explained to me that this would allow for more time to study my case and help to get me acquitted.

This news didn't sit well with me only because I knew I wouldn't be able to go home until I was proven innocent. The thought of being in this cell for who knew how long was depressing, but I knew I had to trust Brad and his knowledge and experience. I cried myself to sleep, and I'm sure I must have kept Thelma up most of the night.

CHAPTER FORTY-SEVEN

It was months before I went to trial. Being in a jail cell for that long was as horrible as I had imagined. I wished I had never been in Sam's store that summer day when I was so young and innocent. Maybe then, Joseph Fletcher wouldn't have cast his dreamy dark eyes on me and seduced this young, naïve girl into his dark, hopeless future.

I was lucky to have Thelma as my cellmate the whole time. She got more comfortable around me after the night I cried myself to sleep, and we became friends and watched each other's backs. I saw and heard horror stories in this jail, where some women were raped and beaten. I had enough of that with Joe...I surely didn't need more of that here. Thelma and I pretty much kept to ourselves and didn't cause any trouble. But prison life changed me. I no longer felt like a sweet, innocent girl. I now had a protective shell around myself and was determined to prove my innocence and get out of this hellhole.

I was glad for the many books I had access to. My family brought me books to pass the time. I started teaching Thelma how to read, and while it was a slow process in the beginning, she finally caught on and was reading every day. Brad also brought me some law books, and I proceeded to learn and educate myself for the days I would be put on trial. I also started writing this journal and will put it in a special, secretive place when I finish writing. I'm sure one day it will be discovered when I'm long gone.

Thankfully, I had lots of visitors during the time I was in prison. Somebody, either Cora, Leo, Mama, Papa, or one of my brothers, was sure to bring Bernice at least once a week. She was a little older now and seemed to accept that her Mama was in a place where she had to stay for a while, but in time, she knew I'd be back home again. She knew a baby brother or sister was in her future, and she was happy and excited for that to happen. I was so thankful that she had so many people in her life to love and care for her in my absence.

CHAPTER FORTY-EIGHT

My pregnancy seemed long and tedious. It felt as if I had been carrying this child forever. But finally, the day came for this baby to be born. It was a Tuesday night, the middle of November, right before midnight that my water broke. I had had pains for a couple of hours but didn't say anything in case it was false labor. When it broke, I called out loudly to the guard on duty. Thelma helped me call out and soon, Horace, the night guard, appeared at the cell door. "What's all the commotion about, ladies?" he asked.

"My water broke," I gasped. "I'm in labor!"

"Well, hold on, then; I'll go tell someone."

"Hurry!" I inhaled sharply.

Soon, a gurney arrived. They opened the door and strapped me down. It was a young, good-looking man who was pushing me toward the medical room. He smiled at me and asked, "Your first?"

I could only grimace and choke out, "Second."

We were in the medical room in minutes. He left, and I was faced with someone I guessed to be the prison doctor. "Well, well, look who's here. The famous husband killer. Now, tell me, Mrs. Fletcher, whose baby will I be delivering today? Will it be a Fletcher or a Hansen?" I'd have kicked him if I could. But I couldn't, so I chose to ignore him. "All right, then, let's see just what's happening down there." I felt humbled and humiliated, but since there was nothing I could do, I stayed silent and let him examine me. Even when the pain was unbearable, I tried not to scream and give him the satisfaction of my suffering.

About an hour later, Evelyn was born. I chose the name Evelyn because I remembered the cutest little girl I went to school with. Her name was Evelyn, but everyone called her "Evie." Besides, it was the female version of Everett, which was my grandfather's name. Now I had two precious girls, and I couldn't wait for Bernice to meet her new little sister.

They made me stay in medical for a couple of days, which I didn't mind because the bed was more comfortable, and I actually had a clean pillow to lay my head on. I looked at Evie and wondered who she looked like. Maybe it was too early to tell because she was still so little, but I couldn't see any resemblance, at least to my side of the family.

They put a cradle in the cell with me and Thelma, and you would have thought I brought Thelma the best gift in the world. While I was worried she would be upset to have a squalling baby with us in the tiny cell, she was overjoyed and insisted on helping with Evie's care. She said she sorely missed her own kids and wasn't even sure what had happened to them, but she assumed they were in orphanages.

Evie was a good baby, but not quite as good as Bernice. She woke every two hours for a feeding and didn't sleep through the night for months. I was exhausted most of the time. Between caring for Evie, visits from family, and meetings with my lawyers, life was crazy and hectic. Bernice fell in love with her little sister. Mama begged me to let her take Evie home to be with them and Bernice, but I refused. Evie was my saving grace…the only thing that made me want to wake up in the morning.

CHAPTER FORTY-NINE

Finally, my trial date was set for June, the year following Otis's July hearing. Evie was seven months old and as adorable as could be. Brad told me that having her in the courtroom would make the jury more sympathetic toward me. He had me dress in widow's black and coached me to just be myself and act calm and intelligent.

I was told that because I was a woman on trial for the murder of my husband, it was sensational news. There were hundreds and hundreds of people gathered around the courthouse. It caused quite a ruckus, and again, I was feeling pity for these people who had nothing better to do. I wondered how many of those people thought I was guilty. Brad told me to try not to let them bother me. They would have nothing to do with my final verdict.

The county courtroom atmosphere was casual. The railings that separated the bench from the jury box and the counsel tables from the court watchers were made of Vermont's polished maple.

The seats in the gallery, behind the bar, according to my brothers, were as hard as most church pews.

Brad informed me that out of almost forty jurors, the state chose five uncompromising people and the defense chose seven genial people. Most of them were middle-aged farmers. Brad told me that he now had the help of a leading law firm from Orange County to assist with my case. They had a lot of experience with criminal cases, and because of the number of lawyers fighting for me, we'd have a good chance to beat this. I thought it must be Papa and Leo paying these professionals' fees, and I was most grateful.

The prosecution was still led by Vermont's Attorney General, Frank Jackson, who was assisted by the new Orange County State's Attorney, Daniel Dunbar. The presiding judge was C. James Conroy.

Mr. Jackson was a serious-looking man. He had a square jaw, a smallish pug-nose, and tight, thin lips that made him look kind of glum. His hair was receding, and it looked as though he grew one side of it long so he could flip it up over his balding head. Brad told me that Jackson had attended Princeton and that he and his assistant, Mr. Dunbar, met there.

One of the interesting facts I learned in reading the law books was that a man only needed to learn law as part of his general curriculum in college or else have been an apprentice to another lawyer in order to practice law. I asked Brad about himself. He said he had indeed learned about law at Litchfield Law School in Connecticut and he also worked under the esteemed attorney, State Senator David S. Conant. I thought that sounded very impressive.

Sugarhouse Trials

The temperature was already in the eighties before noon. It was hot and stuffy in the courtroom, and I could see that Judge Conroy already had beads of sweat on his brow. When he came out and saw the crowds, he ordered that every person who did not have a seat in the courtroom be removed. That took a little while as the deputies escorted the herd back outside. This made me relax a bit. Judge Conroy was a pleasant-looking man, about Papa's age. He had white hair, glasses, and a friendly smile.

The judge proceeded to explain what was about to happen. First, the prosecution would open the case with detailed charges and then show evidence to support these charges. Next would come witnesses for the prosecution, who would be questioned in depth. Then the defense would have their turn.

Jackson told the jurors he would show that I had willfully, knowingly, and with malice conspired with Otis Hansen to go to the sugarhouse and cock, aim, and cold-bloodedly fire a rifle into Joseph Fletcher's brain so that I could be with my lover.

Jackson and Dunbar surprised everyone by calling Otis to the stand as their first witness. His direct testimony was a little different from the confession from his trial. I noticed how calm and careful he was when he spoke. I thought someone may have been coaching him. He still claimed that we were sexually involved and swore that he had no idea that we were going to the sugarhouse to actually kill Joe. *Liar!* I thought. One thing that he did mention, which he hadn't in his confession, was that he had heard Joe and me arguing about whose baby I was carrying. That part was true, as I recalled him following Joe into the barn the day Joe kicked me.

Lenore Sylvain Dexter

I hated to admit I was impressed by Otis, and I thought he was making a good impression on the jurors.

The next witness was Cora, who walked them through that horrible morning we discovered Joe's body. She once again had to tell the story of how Joe didn't sleep in the house that night, how she and Bernice had searched the barn and didn't find him. No, to her knowledge, I had never left the house that night. Yes, it was my idea to go to the sugarhouse. Yes, I had asked her to go in first; yes, I immediately sent her back to the house. No, I didn't cry when I initially told her I thought he was dead. Yes, he physically abused me. No, Joe and I didn't have a happy marriage, and on and on…and every time she tried to explain her yes and no answers, she was cut off and immediately asked a different question. Poor Cora looked at me like she had just taken a shovel and buried me deep in the dirt. I tried to give her a look that said, *Don't worry*, but I don't know if she got it.

Dr. Shepherd was the next witness. He explained in medical terms what his findings were. When he'd first examined the body and declared it a murder, he heard several people saying that I kept insisting that it must have been a suicide. When asked how I'd behaved when I heard Joe had been murdered, he testified that I didn't seem to act shocked or grieve. This made me weep. My lawyers told me to try not to show emotion in court, but being judged by my reaction to Joe's death hit me hard. A little voice inside me said, *If I **had** carried on, they would still be criticizing and accusing me.*

There were minor witnesses brought in the next couple of days to prove motive. People who had seen me bruised, people who knew how bad Joe had become, people who had seen me and Otis alone together...it was emotionally exhausting. I finally consented to let Mama take Evie home with her but made her promise that someone would bring her to court every day so I could see my baby. As much as I missed Evie, it was for the best. I needed the rest and time to concentrate on my trial.

Wilma was called back to the witness stand. When she'd testified for Otis, she claimed he came home at 8:00 the night of the murder and then never left. Now, with scared eyes, she admitted she had made a mistake. She said he left again after 9:00 p.m., and that he didn't return until after 11:00 p.m. Poor Wilma. I couldn't help but feel sorry for this poor woman whose life hadn't been anything but unhappy.

Another witness testified that he saw Otis and me together at the Halloween social, but the judge ruled that whole incident irrelevant. "Mrs. Fletcher isn't on trial for adultery. She's on trial for murder."

I thought, *Thank goodness because that was really nothing.*

When the state rested a week later, my lawyers asked Judge Conroy to remove the case from the jury and issue a verdict of not guilty because it seemed the only evidence against me was from Otis, who was a self-confessed perjurer. Otis had two different stories, and so did his wife. One of Otis's stories stated that we met at the sugarhouse and one that said we met at my house. The first story he told said I told him to bring his rifle with him and meet me there, and the second story he told said we went there together and brought Joe's rifle to do the deed. The lawyers asked the judge, "How can we trust these testimonies when these two witnesses can't even get their stories straight?" The judge refused to remove the case.

My defense team first called Leo. His testimony was that while Joe was very abusive, I would make excuses for his behavior. Yes, he did give me a refresher course on shooting, but it was only in case Joe got too carried away and I needed it to defend myself and my daughter. Yes, he did think Joe was capable of murder because when he was drunk, he was totally out of his mind. No, he didn't think I would ever be capable of murder, unless it was to defend myself or someone I loved. No, I had no feelings for Otis Hansen. Leo told how I felt sorry for Otis and his wife, but there certainly no romantic feelings on my part.

Cora was brought back to the stand for the defense. The lawyers asked her if she'd heard me get up at any time during the night and leave the house. She told the jury that her bedroom was next door to mine and that if I had left, she would have heard something. She testified she heard nothing. Asked if she ever heard me threaten to kill Joe, she replied in the negative. Did she think I would be capable of murder? No, absolutely not.

A surprise witness was Joe's father, Mr. Fletcher. I had no idea he'd come all this way to defend me at my trial. Seeing him made me choke up. Tears ran down my face as I tried to control myself. He testified that I was an excellent wife to his son. He admitted that Joe had many problems after his accident. He told the jury about Joe's past and the wife and son he had lost and how at that time, he saw firsthand Joe's angry and cruel side. He told how once I came into Joe's life, he became a better man until the accident. He explained how I stood by him in spite of everything and to his knowledge, he couldn't imagine that I could or would hurt another living soul, especially not the father of my children. He told the jury he had the utmost respect for me and that he and his wife couldn't have asked for a better wife for their son. He shared how he offered to take Bernice and me back to Louisiana after Joe's death and said that again, he would still present the same offer at this time. It was later that I learned that Mr. Fletcher was the one who brought in the extra team for the defense and paid every penny of their fees.

Then came Alfred and Marie Thurston, who sat near me at Joe's funeral. Alfred and Marie were friends of my parents and had been for years. Two of their boys were about the same age as Lonny and Doug, and they had gone to school together. Their farm was over near Sam's store. They both testified that I had cried and took on badly as they lowered Joe's casket into the ground.

There were many more witnesses that Brad called to the stand to testify to my good character, and I was grateful to all of them.

Brad told me that all in all, we had a good chance. There was no direct evidence against me. It was pretty much just Otis's word.

But next came the scary part...it was my turn to get up on the witness stand.

CHAPTER FIFTY

It was the second week of the trial. I felt awkward and uneasy as I took the stand, knowing all eyes were upon me. I'd had pep talks from Brad, Leo, Mama, Papa, Lonny, Doug, and even Ella. Hold your head high; be composed and sure of yourself.

Mama made me a new black dress and Thelma helped me with my hair. I was coached: show the jurors that you are innocent and that you have nothing to hide or feel guilty about. You didn't kill Joe, and no one can prove that you did. I held my head straight and maintained a relaxed position...except for my fingers. I kept fidgeting with them until Brad finally handed me a fan so I'd stop. I recognized it as Mama's. I was thankful, not only for having something to do with my hands but also because it was unbearably hot in the courtroom.

I explained how I'd lived in West Langford all my life. I met Joe when I was almost fifteen, and we were married two years later.

Lenore Sylvain Dexter

We had a wonderful marriage until Joe had the accident, which changed him. After that, he was incapable of running the farm, so I hired Otis Hansen to help out. Otis became infatuated with me and got carried away with false hopes that I felt the same about him. He went so far as to tell Joe that I was carrying his baby and that we were planning to run away together to New Hampshire. Of course, this was all made up in his mind. The child I was carrying was definitely Joe's baby, and I would never even think of a romantic relationship with Otis. He was delusional. He knew Joe was hitting me, and he hated Joe. More than once I heard him say he wanted to kill Joe. I believed it was only talking and I didn't think he would ever go through with it, but apparently, I was wrong. I told them how he said he could make it look like a suicide. It was never my idea, and I never offered him money to kill Joe. I said I felt bad for Otis, but I never gave him any encouragement.

Next, I was asked why I kept insisting Joe must have committed suicide when it was determined at the sugarhouse that Joe had been murdered. It hit me again in my heart that I was being judged by not reacting like they expected me to. This judgment, again, was unsettling, and I felt my throat constricting. I struggled to tell the jury how my surprise came when I found out he was murdered because at that point in time, I really believed he had taken his own life. I knew how miserable he was and how he felt inadequate as a man, a farmer, a husband, and a father. When I was told it wasn't suicide, but murder, I couldn't comprehend. I refused to believe it. I said, "It was a horrible shock to me; please believe me. I never would I have imagined someone killing Joe. I fainted when I heard the news."

Closing arguments started the next day. Jackson presented to the jury that I was probably having an affair with Otis Hansen and used him to help me get rid of the abusive man who was making my life a living hell. Because if I had not engaged in illicit sexual relations with Hansen, then what possible motive could he have for killing Joe, a crime for which he was convicted?

Brad came back with the fact that Otis Hansen was a liar and fabricator of made-up fantasies. Otis Hansen killed Joe with the hope that with Joe gone, Anna would turn to him. He said, "Anna had many witnesses who told you this man was not a man she was in any way interested in romantically. She tolerated her husband and defended him even though he abused her repeatedly. She is a compassionate, loving mother and a woman who is well-respected. There is no circumstantial evidence whatsoever that proves Anna Fletcher pulled the trigger to kill her husband. The guilty party is already behind bars. Let this good woman go back home to her two young daughters who need her."

With the final arguments heard, Judge Carter charged the jury and it took them only four hours to come back with a verdict of not guilty! I breathed a sigh of relief, letting out a breath I felt I'd been holding for a very long time. I burst into tears and sat down, covering my face with both hands, relieved that this nightmare was finally over. After a moment to compose myself, I stood up, shook hands with my lawyers, and hugged my parents, Leo, and my baby Evie. I thought about letting Mama bring Bernice to the courtroom that day, but just in case I was found guilty, I decided it wouldn't be a good idea. I couldn't wait to get home and hug her, too.

Lenore Sylvain Dexter

I was taken back to my cell at that point, pending my final arrangements for release. It was bittersweet saying good-bye to Thelma. I was going free, but she still had to stay there and endure the punishment for her husband's crime. I wished there was something I could do to help her. I mentioned her case to Brad, and he assured me he would look into her situation and if there was anything he could help with, he would. I promised Thelma I would visit and bring Evie and Bernice for visits. We cried together, although I know she was happy for me. I did fulfill my promise to her and made sure I visited her about once a month, bringing her treats and hugs from my little ones. Brad introduced her to a different lawyer, and he managed to get her sentence reduced.

PART FIVE

CHAPTER FIFTY-ONE

It was a bright, sunny July day when I got to walk back into my home for the first time since my arrest. All my family and friends were there to celebrate my homecoming. I felt light as a feather and free as a bird. No longer would I ever take freedom for granted. Nor would I take for granted the blue skies, the trees, the birdsong, or the sounds and smells of the farm animals and the Vermont air. After most of the people left to go home that day, I ran to the barn, jumped on Kit's back, and rode like the wind. I had missed him so much, and he seemed thrilled to see me too.

Buddy, bless his heart, was still running the farm as best as he could. He and Papa had sold off some of the livestock, which was fine with me. Cora and Bernice, I was told, were a big help to him. Papa, Doug, Leo, and even Lonny and Lewis came by when they could to help with haying and harvesting. I was so grateful for everyone who stuck by me and helped run the farm.

Now that I was a widow and all, Leo was a familiar face at our home. The girls adored him and so did I. I remembered Lonny's words the night I got engaged to Joe about Leo and me. What I had thought at the time was inconceivable, I now realized I should've paid attention to. My brother had some pretty good instincts, and I guess I should have listened.

Leo asked me to marry him two weeks after I got home. I wondered how that would look to friends, family, and neighbors. It seemed quick.

"Anna, you know…I've told you…I have loved you since we were kids and I've always thought we were meant to be together. I promise I'll take good care of you for the rest of my life and never hurt you. Bernice and Evie will be like my own, and I hope we have at least a dozen of our own!"

"Whoa, Leo! Have mercy on a woman! A dozen?! You think I want to be pregnant forever?" He didn't answer in words, just held me in his arms and kissed me like he was ready to start right then.

I talked to Bernice before I said yes to Leo. She was going on ten and was mature for her age. My poor little girl had gone through so much…more than most children her age…at least here in West Langford. She said, "I love Leo, Mama, but what if he has an accident like Papa Joe and gets mean?"

"Oh, baby girl, everyone is different, and everyone reacts differently to things that happen in their lives. Some people are strong, and some people are weak. Papa Joe had big plans for his life and was a very proud man. He didn't know what to do or how to act when he couldn't do what he wanted and needed to do. He felt like a failure and needed to blame someone for what happened to him. It wasn't his fault that he had his accident...that's why they call it an accident. And because it wasn't his fault and because he felt as though he were failing us, it was easier for him to drink his whiskey and drown his sorrows. Unfortunately, Papa's drinking made him mean, and he took it out on us because we reminded him that he failed at taking care of us. Leo is different than your Papa. He's been farming his whole life, and I'm not going to tell you that he *won't* have an accident, but if he did, I think Leo would act differently than Papa Joe. I think Leo would learn to work with his handicap and I believe Leo would do it with a smile."

"So now I'm asking you, Bernice, do you want to give Leo a chance to be your new Papa? A new Papa for you and Evie?"

She hesitated a bit, looking so cute as her brows furrowed. "Yes, Mama, I think I would like to have Leo as my new Papa. Would we live here or on his farm?"

Well, this was something *I* hadn't even thought of. "Where would you like to live, Bernice?"

"I think maybe Leo's farm...I don't want Papa Joe coming around to ruin everything."

"Okaaaaaayyyyy, baby," I said slowly, "Papa Joe can't come back. You know he died." I thought this was a strange remark. Did she think Joe would come back to haunt us? "I'll talk to Leo, and I'm sure we can sell this farm and move over to Leo's if that makes you feel better."

"Yes, Mama. I love you, Mama. Thanks for giving me a baby sister. I kinda like Evie."

I smiled, "I kinda like Evie too, baby girl."

Leo came over that evening, and I told him about my conversation with Bernice. "She said that? She thinks Joe will still come around? That's creepy."

"I know…I kinda got a chill when she said that."

CHAPTER FIFTY-TWO

Leo and I were married on September 30, 1918. Again, I had a very small, intimate wedding with family only. Bernice had just turned ten and Evie was almost one, toddling around and acting like she was some kind of queen. Bernice was such an easygoing child. She accepted the fact that Evie was in need of most of the attention and catered to her every whim.

I was able to sell our farm to a family who was relocating from Connecticut. They told us that they didn't necessarily want to farm, but they wanted horses and loved the look of my house and outbuildings. With the money from my farm, Leo and I were in a pretty good financial position. Leo's father had passed a couple of years ago, but his mother was still living. She decided to go live with her daughter, Marion, in upstate New York shortly thereafter.

Once again, I was in a state of bliss. I had a loving husband and two beautiful girls, and life was good. I still wondered why

God had put Joe in my life and why I had to go through hell to get where I was today. It seemed like wasted years of my life.

Not long before we were married, the war had broken out. One day, while I was cleaning the chicken coop, a strange man came to visit Leo. They were in the cow barn for what seemed like hours. When Leo finally came in to eat supper, I asked, "What was that about? Who was that guy?"

Leo looked uncomfortable. "Umm...he was a recruiter, Anna. I want to join the Army...it's my duty as an American to fight for our freedom."

"Leo!! What?? We just got married!! Let somebody else go to war! The girls and I need you!"

Leo took my face in his hands and looked deeply into my eyes. "Anna, I have to do this. Trust me."

For the next month, I tried to talk Leo out of his decision. He told me time and time again that it was too late. He had already made the commitment. The only way he could get out of it was if he had an accident and wasn't physically or mentally able to fulfill his duty. Well, of course, he knew I didn't want *that* to happen. It was a sad time for me, anticipating his being gone. I truly could not understand his thinking.

We talked Buddy and Cora into helping us out at our farm from time to time while Leo was gone. They were both getting up in years and were both at the point in their lives where they were ready to slow down. I only called upon them for help when absolutely needed, but I always called upon them for family dinners and visits. Our children were like their grandchildren, and they were always ready and willing to come when they were invited.

Sugarhouse Trials

Leo left the next month. It was a Monday morning, and Doug offered to take him to the train station. When he learned that Leo had enlisted, Doug also followed suit, and Mama shared my anxious feelings. I still had a hard time accepting their decisions. We were all feeling sad as we watched them load up his belongings. He climbed into the car and looked out at us. Bernice and I were trying to be brave, but we both had tears streaming down our faces. Little Evie didn't know what was going on, but instead of her happy little face, she looked quite serious. He waved good-bye and we waved back, and then he was gone.

The girls and I missed him terribly. It was like there was something missing in our lives…an empty hole to complete our days. Buddy and Cora's presence in our lives was a true blessing. Mama and Papa were, thankfully, back in our lives full time, and once again, Sundays were a treasured day for us as the whole family gathered in their country kitchen to enjoy Mama's delicious meals. I was glad the girls were reunited with all their cousins, and it was almost as if my scandalous past had never existed.

About a month after Leo left, I knew I was once again with child. Leo would be so happy. I was able to correspond with him by mail but wasn't sure how long it took for him to receive my news. He was stationed in France, so very far away. I told him in my letters that his wishes were coming true and that he would be a Papa in six months. I wondered if he would be home and in my arms soon after that to start on another child. This time, I was secretly hoping for a boy.

CHAPTER FIFTY-THREE

Just when you think all is well and life is bliss, it changes once again. Tragedy came right after Leo left. Papa was in the barn milking their only cow early one morning and dropped dead. Mama found him lying on the floor with his hand clutching his chest. The doctor was sent for and said it was probably Papa's heart that gave out. Mama took it bad. I convinced her to come stay with the girls and me, at least for a while, until she decided what she wanted to do with the farm since Doug had also left for the Army. We weren't quite sure where he was or when he was coming back. "Good Ol' Buddy" said he would be sure to go at least once a day to tend to her few animals and help out whenever he was needed. I suggested she sell the farm and come live permanently with me, Leo, and the girls, but she wanted to hold out on that until Doug got back. I was relieved, though, when Mama agreed to at least live with us for the time being. The girls would be a distraction for her, and she wouldn't be lonely in a big house by herself.

Not long after that, Bernice came down with a nasty cold. I kept her home from school for a week, thinking all she needed was rest and lots of soup. After a week, though, she wasn't getting any better. I sent for Doc Shepherd when she became feverish. He told me to keep cold rags on her forehead and keep trying to give her soup. Between Mama, Cora and me, she had twenty-four-hour care, but it didn't do any good. My sweet baby girl died one night from scarlet fever in her sleep. I was inconsolable. Mama wasn't much better. It was as if a big, black cloud had been hovering over our lives since the day Leo left. I took to my bed for days and didn't want to leave it. I had no appetite and felt like I was in a deep, dark hole and couldn't find my way out. Mama, Cora, and even Buddy tried to coax me out of my deep depression, but it was as though I were paralyzed. I didn't even want to live. I wanted to escape and sleep in peace.

One early spring afternoon, as I lay lifeless in the bed that had become my black nest, the bedroom door opened. "Anna, can you hear me?" I thought I was dreaming because it sounded like Leo. I felt a warm hand on my cheek. "Anna, wake up...I'm home. Evie and I—and that little baby of ours you are carrying—need you." I knew I had to be dreaming. Slowly, I opened my eyes.

"Am I dreaming, Leo, or are you truly here?"

"I'm truly here, my love, and I'm not leaving you ever again if I can help it."

I tried to sit up and he saw my struggle. "Here, let me help you." Very gently, he sat me up and placed two pillows behind me for support. Then he sat on the edge of the bed, held me, and

Sugarhouse Trials

started crying. We sat like that together for a bit, both crying our hearts out for Bernice.

Leo saved me and our baby boy. Baby Leo Jr. was born on May 25. He was born a little premature because I wasn't taking care of myself. Leo couldn't believe how thin I was. All my clothes hung on me as if they were two sizes too big. The baby was only five pounds, and I was thankful that even though he was tiny, the doctor said he seemed perfectly healthy. I tried to explain to Leo that the feelings I was having when I lost Bernice were beyond my control. I had given up and was ready to die. I just didn't have the strength, physically or mentally, to be there for Evie and my mother.

"Leo, you have to know I would never do anything to purposely hurt our unborn baby." I tried to explain to him that it was like my body and mind had been taken over by a dark force that was so strong I couldn't fight it. I hoped and prayed I would never feel that despair ever again.

Some men would have blamed me for being weak and selfish. Leo blamed himself for leaving us, but I assured him that it had nothing to do with his leaving. I was just so very happy that he was home and here to take care of us.

I found out later that Cora had written to Leo and told him all that was going on. I don't know how he did it, but he convinced some higher-ups in the Army for a general discharge. He again apologized that he had ever consented to leave us, but when that recruiter came around, he'd spent a lot of time with Leo making him feel it was his duty to fight for our country. I didn't care. I was just happy he was back home.

Some people say that bad things happen in threes. I tend to think there may be something to that. The very next year, we laid Mama to rest in a grave beside Papa. She never got over losing him and Bernice so close together. I think seeing Leo and me as a happy couple only made her feel her loss of Papa more keenly. Doug was also discharged but wasn't interested in farming anymore. He decided to sell The Hermitage and split the profit among the four of us kids. We all somberly packed up Mama and Papa's belongings, took what we wanted out of the big, beautiful house with so many fond memories, and sold it to a wealthy businessman from New York. He said it was to be his summer house and offered to hire Doug to be a caretaker. It was a good offer, and Doug readily accepted.

Cora and Buddy lived to be in their eighties. While they were still living, we always included them as part of the family. I never forgot how they loved and supported Bernice and me during all of my many dark days. We always made sure they were well taken care of since we were their only family.

CHAPTER FIFTY-FOUR

Leo and I had a good life and many happy years together. When Leo came back from France, he confided in me that he no longer wanted to be a full-time farmer. "Oh, I'll still keep a few cows, maybe a couple three pigs and our chickens, Anna, but I think I'd like to try to earn a living as a blacksmith instead."

"That's fine with me, Leo, but I didn't know you knew that trade."

"I never mentioned it to you, but while you were away, I spent quite a bit of time with our town blacksmith, Floyd Dubois. He's getting up there in years and asked me if I'd like to learn the trade and maybe take over his business when he retired. After spending two weeks learning with him, I decided I liked it and continued going to the blacksmith forge for experience. When you came back, I told him I would think about his offer and talk it over with you. Then I decided to join the Army and didn't give it much thought until I was headed back home. On the long trip back, I had plenty of time to think. So, if it's okay with you, I'd like to try my hand at it."

"Well, it sounds like a new beginning, Leo, and I'm all for new beginnings. Where's his shop?"

"Well, it's over on the outskirts of town, but I was thinking of building my own forge here on the property. I figure if I build a big garage, I could set up shop right here so I could be close to you and the kids every day. You know I like working with my hands and I love carpentry, so I'd like to get started on building right quick."

"Okay, Leo. You definitely have my support."

Leo worked long hours on that garage. It ended up being a six-bay garage, and all the neighbors were in awe. Nobody in West Langford had anything like it. When he was done, Floyd came over, and they negotiated prices for equipment. It didn't take long for word to spread and before we knew it, Leo had quite a business for himself. I was pretty proud of him.

Not only was he the town blacksmith now, but he also ran and got elected as town selectman. Leo had lots of good ideas for our little town and because he was so well-liked by everyone, most of his ideas were well received.

Yes, Leo was a jack-of-all-trades, all right. He started painting houses, and at one point, he took up real estate. He bought up old homes, fixed them up, and resold them for a profit. When the grandsons came along, he taught them lots of different skills that they'd be able to use throughout their lives. He had a way with the kids and they adored him…just like Mary's kids had years ago. Kids and animals. We had this one pup named Poochie. He was just a

Sugarhouse Trials

small black-and-white mutt, but he loved Leo. When Leo would leave in his old pickup truck, Poochie would follow the truck for about a mile down the road. It was comical to see because he always stopped at Irma Flatt's house, lay down at the end of her drive, and waited for Leo to come back. Leo would stop the truck, Poochie would jump in, and Leo would drive him back home. That was something!

We did end up having a large family with 11 kids. I pretty much had one a year, and life was never dull in the Decker family. All the children had different personalities, and we took joy in them. From age three, they learned responsibility by doing small chores around the farm. They were good kids and seemed well-liked by everyone in town.

With large families, though, sometimes you're more likely to have tragedy. Leo and I had five girls and six boys together. When our son Glen was sixteen, he worked at a gas station pumping gas. While he was servicing a customer one day, the very stupid person threw his cigarette out of the vehicle. There was gasoline on the ground, and it immediately ignited. Glen didn't stand a chance. Both he and the customer died that day. Leo and I grieved for a very long time, as did all our children.

That wasn't the end of the tragedy in our lives. Our son Douglas decided to enlist and serve in World War II. He never came back. He was a war hero, and although we were very proud of him, I couldn't help but wish we'd never let him go to war. It's very hard to lose a child; it's doubly hard to lose two children, but I had lost three of them. It seemed to me it was more than my share. But that's life, and so often we have no control over it. We take what's given us and cope the best way we can.

CHAPTER FIFTY-FIVE

Dinnertimes were always the highlights of my day when the children were young. With eleven kids, someone always had a story to tell. Leo was quite the handyman and made us a big country dining room table from the maple trees he cut down on our property. It was practically the whole length of our kitchen, but we needed it big so we could all fit around it. There was always laughter and teasing and everyone talking at once. I always made it a point to really look at my children and talk to each one alone every day because I remembered Miss Everdeen as the teacher who would take time with each of her students individually. I knew that time went fast, and it wouldn't be long before they would grow up, leave, and start families of their own. I remembered what Doc Hayes' wife, Grace, told Leo and me years ago about being proud of children who grow up to be good, God-fearing, responsible adults. I also remembered Leo's words at Mary's. "We'd make some pretty fine parents someday, Anna." I guess Leo was right.

When the grandchildren started coming, it was a whole new experience for me. I loved being a mother, but being a grandmother was even better. I was able to love them and spoil them and send them home when I got tired. Leo was an excellent Grampa. He had the ability to teach them many things, not only work-related but about life, too. His favorite saying to them was, "Do what you do, do well." It was something he lived by, and I was glad he passed it on to his kids and grandkids. I knew the grandkids loved us as much as we loved them because one or another was always at our home. We were never alone. Every holiday, we would rent the Grange Hall and have our family celebrations. We would all pitch in to help organize, decorate, cook, and bake. Each and every year, the kids and all the grandkids tried to make it a point to attend. All Mama's recipes were put to use, and our holiday banquets were the talk of the town.

CHAPTER FIFTY-SIX

As the years went by, I watched our little town of West Langford change before my eyes. I thought about how lucky I was to witness all the new innovations of the time. We now had indoor plumbing, and laundry was so much easier with washing machines. Most of my kids had electric dryers, too. There were airplanes that could take you from state to state in a matter of hours. I thought of the trip I took with Joe and Bernice by train and how long it had taken to get to Louisiana and back. Everyone had a car now, and some people had two! We had televisions that could show us what was happening all around the world. There were shopping malls where you could buy anything your heart desired. It was a new way of living. Life was easier by far, and I was glad for my grandchildren. But I was also glad that Leo and I were here to experience this new way of living.

CHAPTER FIFTY-SEVEN

Leo decided to retire when he was about sixty-five. When he first retired, he was lost as to what to do with all his free time, but that didn't last long. I encouraged him to pursue his woodworking since I saw what talent he had when he built our dining table. He spent hours in the barn and made quite a few pieces of furniture…some we kept, and some we gave to the kids. We still had some chickens around because I wanted fresh eggs, so I took responsibility for them. I still baked bread every week as well as lots of desserts, as Leo had a sweet tooth. We still had our apple orchard, and the kids always enjoyed picking apples in the fall. They told me I made a pretty good apple pie, so they made it a point to always bring me a bushel. The grandkids always knew Grammy would have some kind of treat for them to enjoy.

CHAPTER FIFTY-EIGHT

It was one of the saddest days of my life when Leo passed. He and I had been best friends forever. It was a week before my seventy-ninth birthday. He had been ill for the past year, so we were all kind of expecting he wouldn't be with us much longer. Even though you know you are about to lose someone, it doesn't make it any easier when they finally take their last breath. Toward the end, one by one, every grandchild came to sit with him, taking turns day after day keeping him company as he lay in his bed. One night, he told me, "Anna, thank you for making my life complete. I couldn't have asked for a better wife and family. We made some pretty amazing kids, and they blessed us with these beautiful grandkids who take time out of their young lives to come sit with me. How blessed are we?" I couldn't agree more.

Leo and I never talked about the past. Looking back, it seemed like more of a nightmare than a reality. I think most of the people who knew about the incident were dead or just plain forgot about it. I was just as glad. Papa used to tell me what's passed is in the past. Forget about it and move on.

Life without Leo just isn't the same. I decided today to end this journal I've been writing for years. Even though I'm almost eighty, I have decided to stay at my house. All nine of my children offered for me to come live with them, but this is my home, and as long as I am able to care for myself, I'm staying put. As I said, it's no longer a working farm and hasn't been for some time. I pretty much stay downstairs because my kids don't want me going up and down the stairs. Some of the boys brought my bedroom set down to one of the back rooms. It's convenient because off that room is my bathroom, complete with toilet, sink, and bathtub. I'm content right now, although I do miss Leo every day and every night. My big old bed is lonely now with just me in it.

If anyone should find and read this journal, I pray they will think of me as a good and loving person because I do believe God has blessed me with lots of love to give away. I only hope I was generous enough…

EPILOGUE

My room is getting darker and I am getting weaker. My visiting nurse will be coming in soon with my dinner, and I'm guessing my granddaughter will be joining me a little later, as she has been doing the last couple of days. I wonder what she would think of her sweet Grammy if she really knew the truth of what happened in the sugarhouse that night. When she reads my journal, she will assume that Otis killed Joe and I was innocent. It's a strange feeling to know that your life is about to end. But I know it as well as I know the sun is going to rise every morning, with or without me.

As I said, my life was blessed and I had many good things in my life, but before I die in these last moments on Earth, I feel the need to pray and ask for forgiveness from the God I was told was merciful. Now is the time to confess before I take my last breath. I thought of asking Anna to fetch me the pastor, but I know it would upset her too much. If I were to confess, I would tell him part of my life *was* a lie. If you would have told me my future and what I was capable of when I was a young mother, I would have scoffed at you and told you that you were crazy. But here I am, an eighty-five-year-old woman, knowing what really happened that night at the sugarhouse—and so now, on this deathbed of mine, I'm finally ready to admit the truth to myself and to God, priest or no priest.

If you tell the same lie over and over again for years, you finally believe it as being true. I refused to believe and admit the truth for so long, that I truly had myself believing I *was* innocent in Joe's death and that Otis was totally responsible.

To be honest, I have no idea who Evie's real father is.

Once Joe started to hit me, I knew that wasn't what marriage was supposed to be like. After the accident, Joe was a totally different person, and I fell out of love with him. I was so frustrated and angry when he hit me because I couldn't defend myself. He was so much stronger than I was. That was bad enough. But when he started having his way with me and I couldn't fend him off, I felt like a total victim. What kind of mother figure was I giving my daughter? My parents were the ultimate example of a happy, well-adjusted marriage, and the union between Joe and me was nothing but sick and unhealthy. I couldn't have Bernice live day after day with the hostility between Joe and me.

No one ever suspected (except Joe…and I always denied it) that I used to take Kit and sneak off to Leo's house whenever I could. I needed to feel true love and affection. It started off innocent enough, with me just venting, but one thing led to another and when he put his arms around me and confessed his love in words, it was like a whiskey high. When I was with Leo, I was in the moment and was able to forget all the hurt and anguish I experienced at home. I loved Leo and knew that the love we felt for each other was right and healthy.

Then there was Otis. The confession Otis presented at our trials had more truth than fiction. The first time Otis came on to me, I felt revulsion. There was no way I would consent to his advances. He wasn't attractive to me whatsoever, but once Joe started taking me by force, it was more than I could handle. I was thinking of myself, but more so of my daughter. Thinking about Wilma's sad story, I was afraid that Joe would start on Bernice once she was a little older. Joe seemed totally out of his mind when he was drinking. At that point, much to my shame, I decided to use Otis. I noticed how he looked at me with lust and I knew it would be easy to do because he would be easy to manipulate. I thought about it long and hard and decided it was the only way I could be free of Joe and still be a good example of a mother to Bernice. If Otis killed Joe, I could live my life free of abuse, and Bernice and I would be happy and free of fear. This was not something I was proud of or wanted to do, but I truly was desperate.

One day, when Otis and I were in the barn together, I took his hand and led him behind a pile of hay. I kissed him on the lips, and it went on from there. I felt the power and now had him under my thumb. I had to close my eyes when I was with him because he really did repulse me, but I rationalized my actions for Bernice and for my survival. He told me he would do anything for me, and I believed him. We had sex once a week so I could keep a handle on him. It made me feel like the whore Joe accused me of being, but I kept telling myself it was for Bernice's and my future.

The evening Joe threw the stew pot at my feet was the straw that broke the camel's back. Once Joe left for the sugarhouse and Cora and Bernice tended to my swollen foot, I told them I was going to bed. Once they were settled, I snuck out and limped to the Hoods' guesthouse. I was afraid to take Kit because we might be seen if we met someone on the road. On foot, I could hide if need be. I knocked on the door, and Wilma answered it. She immediately slammed the door in my face. I heard heated words inside, and soon enough, Otis came through the door. He looked down at my foot, which I had hanging in the air because it was hurting so badly. "Hey, Anna, are you okay?" he asked, concerned. "What's wrong with your foot?"

I ignored his question and whispered, "Otis, I think the time has come. We have to plan for Joe's suicide. Are you still with me on this?"

I could see the desire in his eyes. "Oh, yes, Anna; I'm with you all the way. What's the plan?"

"Well, I'm not quite sure yet, but when the time is right, I'll be sure to let you know. I just want to be sure you're still willing to help me."

"Well, of course, Anna; I would do anything for you, ya know? I told you that."

"All right, then, go back to Wilma and you'll be hearing from me."

"Okay, Anna," he replied with desire in his eyes. "While you're here, you wanna have a little fun behind the big oak tree?"

Trying to control my facial expression, I replied, "Sorry, Otis, gotta get back to Bernice...but soon." I questioned myself, *What am*

I doing? I remember saying to myself, *Don't think, Anna...this is something that needs to get done.*

I knew Wilma sometimes went to Mabel's sewing circle on Saturdays, so when Joe took off to go to Sam's for supplies the day of his death, I went to find Otis. I found him outside of one of the Hoods' barns sharpening a handsaw. He looked up in surprise when he saw me. "Anna, you're here! I was jes thinking of ya."

"Otis, tonight is the night. I need you to meet me at our sugarhouse around eleven o'clock tonight. Bring your rifle. Can you do that?"

"Anna, how many times do I have to tell you? I'd do anything for ya. I'll be there."

"Okay, Otis; I'm counting on you." And as much as I hated myself for doing it, I kissed him good, securing our deal, and hurried away before he suggested anything more.

That Saturday night, I begged off early, telling Cora and Bernice that my foot hurt and I was going to bed early to rest it. I dozed off from time to time but made sure I was awake enough to know when the two of them went to bed and closed the door. I carefully snuck out and put my sweater and Joe's old boots on since the path to the sugarhouse was still covered with snow. Besides, his boots were the only comfortable footwear I could tolerate because of my swollen foot.

I got to the sugarhouse before Otis did. I peeked through the small, round knothole in the side of the house. I could see Joe passed out, his head down on his chest, his legs splayed out and his arms relaxed on his lap. Now **was** the time, I thought. *Where the heck is Otis?* Just then, I heard a rustling nearby.

"Otis, that you?" I whispered.

"Yeah, Anna, it's me."

"You have your rifle?"

"Yes, Anna; I've got it right here."

"Well, come on, then...see this here hole in the wall? You can just put the rifle barrel in it and shoot...it should hit Joe right where it needs to be."

"Anna, ya really wanna do this? I'm not so sure it's such a good idea. I didn't really think you would actually go through with this." He was acting like a skittish horse and was whispering much too loudly.

"Otis!! Shhhh..." I whispered. "Keep it down! Are you betraying me? ... You told me you were with me on this. You told me many times that you would do anything for me. I need you to do this! Now!" I felt as skittish as he was acting but was determined to get the deed done.

"Sorry, Anna, I really kinda thought you was bluffing, ya know? I don't think we should do this," he said in his slow-witted way.

I was so angry and so upset and so out of control, I said, "Give me that rifle!!" And without another thought, I aimed it through that little hole in the wall and took the shot. Otis took off like a rocket and ran. I wasn't even sure if my shot was accurate, but I carefully and slowly entered the sugarhouse. I really and truly didn't know if Joe was dead, but he was slumped on the chair, so I pushed him down on the floor and took Otis's rifle and placed it under his body. Then I hobbled back to the house.

I snuck in and got into bed as quietly as I could. *Did I really just shoot Joe?* Was he dead? What was going to happen? Did anyone hear the gunshot? Would people suspect me? Would Otis tell on me? So many questions ran through my mind. I dozed off a couple of times, but never really slept. It was a very long night.

Strangely, I did feel shock and pain when I found out the next day that Joe was really dead. I was in such shock that for a while, I blocked out the fact that it was me who killed him.

When I finally realized and remembered what happened, I became a good liar and a good actress. I thought when Otis was arrested, that I was off the hook, but when Leo came to tell me that Otis was telling everyone it was me who killed Joe, I started to panic. I knew I had to find "strong Anna" somewhere deep inside me...not only for myself, but for my children. So, I started convincing myself that I was innocent and that Otis was just making up stories to save himself. I was shocked when he told the jury that I made him move Joe and he was the one to place the rifle under him. I guess in his dim-witted way, Otis was trying to protect me a little and prove his love for me. Who knows? But like I said, if you tell yourself a lie enough times, you really do start to believe it. Somehow, I also managed to convince my family and friends, and even a jury, that I was innocent and Otis was the guilty party who actually shot and killed Joe. Otis was in jail with a life sentence. It was something I thought I would have to live with for the rest of my life. Thankfully, years later, I heard he had been pardoned by the governor for reasons I never knew.

I never talked about my past life to my children or my grandchildren. To them, I was the sweetest, most loving grandmother they could ever ask for and Leo was the only man in my life. Leo was the only one who really knew the truth, and I knew my secret was safe with him. I told him the whole story one evening before I even went to jail. He then told me that if Otis hadn't agreed to help me, he would have been with me to help end Joe's life. God help us both.

I wish I could say that I regretted what I did, but once Joe was out of my life, I was a much happier person. With Leo as my husband and father to all of our children, they were able to live a normal, happy childhood. Evie was much older when she found out Leo wasn't her real father. I'm not sure who told her, but it wasn't anyone in my family. She confronted me, and I told her that although Leo may not be her biological father, he was certainly the *only* father she ever had.

Now I think I'm ready to close my eyes for the last time. I'm so very tired and ready to leave this life and join Leo. *May God have mercy on my soul...*

ACKNOWLEDGMENTS

I would like to thank my friend and editor, Tamara Beach, who gave me the encouragement to write a novel. Also, my dear friends and family, Jaime, Johanna, my two Nancys, Peggy, and of course my Mom, who all supported and urged me to publish.

ABOUT THE AUTHOR

Sugarhouse Trials is Lenore Sylvain Dexter's first novel. She found her creative voice in retirement writing incredibly compelling historical fiction. She and her husband, Joe, live in Tucson, AZ with their dog, Rigby.

Made in the USA
Las Vegas, NV
17 April 2021